PERFECT STRANGERS

A STORY BY SOMYA PANDEY

BLUEROSE PUBLISHERS
India | U.K.

Copyright © Somya Pandey 2024

All rights reserved by author. No part of this publication may be reproduced, stored in a retrieval system or transmitted in any form or by any means, electronic, mechanical, photocopying, recording or otherwise, without the prior permission of the author. Although every precaution has been taken to verify the accuracy of the information contained herein, the publisher assume no responsibility for any errors or omissions. No liability is assumed for damages that may result from the use of information contained within.

BlueRose Publishers takes no responsibility for any damages, losses, or liabilities that may arise from the use or misuse of the information, products, or services provided in this publication.

For permissions requests or inquiries regarding this publication, please contact:

BLUEROSE PUBLISHERS
www.BlueRoseONE.com
info@bluerosepublishers.com
+91 8882 898 898
+4407342408967

ISBN: 978-93-5989-966-4

Cover design: Kaustubh Vichare
Typesetting: Tanya Raj Upadhyay

First Edition: February 2024

ACKNOWLEDGMENT

TO RAAHI

2018

My best friend, Karan Bhojkar, and I were chilling in his Railway colony when he told me about a girl who used to be his neighbor back then. That's when he came up with the idea of "Perfect Strangers."

Although the story is completely different, I will always be grateful to him for initiating this idea.

2020

After the demise of my Nana, who was also a writer and a poet, I decided to convert the story into a novel.

I started writing the story, and that's how those two unnamed characters became Ahilya and Yohanne.

Thanks to the person who inspired the backstory of Yohanne. Also, thanks to the couples around me with so many relationship problems, which helped me understand how love stories in real life work.

I would like to thank my family for being so supportive of the book.

Thanks to Kaustubh for making me feel confident enough to finish the story and for creating the beautiful cover.

I would also like to thank the publishing team and Mansi, especially for making it possible in such a short span of time.

The story was with me for such a long time, but I finally got the strength to present it.

I hope every girl can relate to the story and decide if they want to pick their Rahil or find their Yohanne.

Lastly, I want to express my gratitude to Pakhi, my 9-year-old cousin, who had faith in my story – a story she had never heard but somehow understood. Her words will always stick with me when she said, "I will read this book when I find my Yohanne."

PERFECT STRANGERS

What is love? It's something I've learned from my Dad's one and only novel, 'Ek Aag Ka Dariya Hai.' I wonder at times why he didn't try writing again. What's not love? It's something I've seen at home. Even though I love the way he has written the book, I've never finished it.

You must be thinking, why not? It's because the book is based on my parents' love story, Zaid and Shraddha's love story, and the publishers believed that the perfect end to this beautiful tale would not be a "happily ever after" but the death of our hero. You know, deaths are glorified in love for some reason, but I get it. When you get your love, you stop valuing it and eventually lose it. But if you die, your love freezes and stays the way it was, forever and ever. Zaid dies, and Ahilya does not exist in that book. But here she is, with a story of her own. Well, let's accept that Gen-Z can't understand what love actually is. But this is the closest I've ever been to love.

CHAPTER 1

Ahilya

I was sitting in my usual cafe, 'Coffee Craft,' waiting for Rahil, and even though I knew that the glass window was covered with fog and droplets, I kept looking out, as if I could see through it. The café wasn't so crowded, I looked at the books on the wooden rack. There were multiple famous books but it didn't have my dad's book. There were times when I wanted to tell the café manager to put up my dad's book too but I realised it was too personal and I wouldn't like it either. I looked outside again, I couldn't help but think that if the rain didn't stop, my shoes might get wet, and I wouldn't be able to wear them again tomorrow. I'll have to pack these wet shoes into a plastic bag, and it'll be a lot of work that I didn't want to do. I looked around; the café was starting to get full.

As I was waiting for Rahil, I noticed a couple sitting at the table in front of me. The girl had finished her drink, and the guy was only halfway there. The girl was extremely pretty, but the guy looked creepy—rich but creepy. The girl didn't seem interested in his conversation, but he kept talking. I looked back at the window.

I saw a figure like Rahil through those blurry windows, and my heart started racing. I didn't know if I was planning on doing the right thing or not, but I knew that I would go through with it. Rahil was a 6'2 inches tall guy; he had dimples when he smiled, and his hair was a little curly, things would always get stuck in his hair.

He entered, and like an instinct, I stood up to hug him. "How are you?" he asked. "Good." There was a very sweet smile on his face when he held me. When I hugged him, I realized that I was correct.

I didn't love him. He pulled a chair and sat right in front of me, placing his hands on the table and looking right into my eyes. His face looked as beautiful as always, which reminded me that I hadn't asked him back if he was doing good or not. He looked fine to me. After that ugly argument last night, I thought he would be a little angry or at least not this fine.

"So what do you wanna have?" he asked, looking at the menu. Why was he even looking at the menu? I mean, we went there every week, and still, he was pretending to see what's new? Like he was avoiding eye contact. "Just order the usuals na," I looked straight at him so that he could stop pretending. He stood up to place the order; yes, 'Coffee Craft' was one of those places where you have to go and place your order. He got in the queue and kept turning and looking at me; I smiled at him, but not the one that gives someone reassurance, the one that says I feel bad for whatever is happening. He didn't smile back. He turned his head to the barista and placed his order. He was wearing the same shirt I had gifted him.

He was so happy that day, and I remember I gave it to him as a return gift for the anklet he got me. I didn't even remember where that anklet was.

He walked back to our table, and I took a deep breath. I was going to start with the speech I had planned while waiting for him, but he started talking. "I know it will be very difficult to manage long distance, but trust me, Pune isn't that far, and I can come to see you every weekend," he said, trying to convince me.

"I know, but you will travel 3 hours and then meet me for a couple of hours and then travel back 3 hours? I can't let you do this." "I want to do this," he said, making that pleading face, and he held my hand with his warm, soft fingers. "You will do this, but till when? One fine day, you will be done and exhausted, and then you will blame me for that, and I will always be under this guilt that I am making you do all this for me." He pulled my hand closer to him.

"That won't happen," he kissed my fingers. "Why are you making it so difficult, Rahil?" I took my hand away from his grip. He looked down at it and then straight back at me. I wanted to just disappear for that moment, but I knew that it was for the best.

The waiter came to our table and placed two glasses of Kitkat shakes on our table. Yes, that was our usuals. I slid one glass towards him and took one for me.

He kept looking at me, and his expressions were changing slowly; he looked frustrated and a little mad at me. I felt bad for making him go through all this, but at that moment, I really wanted a sip of that shake. I didn't have it in me to look at him, so I kept looking at the shake, the way drops were sliding down the glass, and it got so silent that I could focus on the sound of rain coming from outside. I shifted my focus to the song that was being played inside the cafe.

'Could you find a way to let me down slowly?' Why the hell would they play this song?

"You won't change your mind?" he asked and stared deep into my eyes. I started fidgeting with the tissue box on our table. I took a tissue out and wiped the water off my glass.

"I tried for too long, and we started dating like a year ago, to be honest I didn't even know what I was feeling, for the first time a guy, as good looking as you, did something to impress me, you know, I just could not say no." I said

"what do you mean?" he asked leaning towards me. this is something I had kept inside for too long. I never wanted to tell him that when I agreed to be his girlfriend, I wasn't in love with him.

I took a deep breathe before answering that question.

"what I mean is that when you asked me to be your girlfriend, I could not say no."

"No, that I got, what I am asking is Ahilya, you are saying that you never loved me?" he asked, I could see anger in his eyes, anger and disbelief. Like he just wanted me to deny everything I had just mentioned.

"I can't call it love." I mumbled, avoiding the eye contact.

"Look at me Ahilya." He said slightly banging the table with his fist.

"Look Rahil, can you please stop creating a scene, It's not like I didn't try, I tried falling in love with you for the whole year." I said and looked at him, his eyes were a little red.

"You tried but I got attached, what about me now? You're using long distance to end this but what about me." he asked, and his tone softened.

I had nothing to say. I knew if I utter one more word I will start crying here. We both didn't say anything for a while.

"Okay, let's get this over with then," he said suddenly, and I looked at him, raising my eyebrows as I had no clue where he was going with the sentence. He looked down while speaking, and I knew why. He couldn't look at me while saying what he was going to.

"I love you, but you don't love me enough to fight for me, you.. you didn't even love me to begin with. so it's better we finish this. I will not try more, but I will not even wish anything bad for you, Ahilya. I hope you get what you want," he looked at me as he finished speaking.

Suddenly my throat felt heavy, like I was about to cry. His eyes were already wet. He held my hand again and kissed it. He stood up, took a last look at me, and walked away. My heart did ask me to stop him, but stopping him would just be a temporary solution, and we both would have to go through this again.

He didn't even drink his Kitkat shake.

It hurt really bad, and I realized why my parents never left each other. For them, holding on was easier than letting go.

I took my phone out of my bag and dialed my best friend's number.

"Yeah, I did it; can you come and pick me? It's still raining outside." I felt numb, but to be very honest, there was a sense of peace in that pain. Like this was something I wanted. I wanted to feel this kind of pain.

Didn't know why.

"Will be there in 5 minutes," Kajal said. I started drinking that shake, and I started feeling okay. I saw that couple, and the girl was still listening to him. I sighed and looked outside. Rahil was standing there in the rain. I could have gone outside, maybe hugged him and told him that I wanted to be with him. But I did not want to be with him; it wasn't love that I was feeling for him. Not the kind of love my Dad wrote about. I took a sip from my drink and looked back at the window; he was gone. The door opened, and I saw Kajal and Abhishek walking in. Kajal, as always, looked really hot, and I still don't know how Abhishek pulled her off, but he is also a very sweet guy. They looked a little mismatched, but I loved them to death. She sat next to me, and Abhishek sat on the chair where Rahil was sitting. Kajal patted on my shoulders and Abhishek was looking at the kitkat shake without even blinking "You can drink that; he didn't even touch it."I said

"No no, I'm good," he looked at the glass again.

"Please drink it, Abhi; it will go to waste otherwise," Kajal said, and he smiled at me. I looked at Kajal, who was staring at him with pettiness in her eyes. I couldn't help but chuckle, and Kajal smiled too. He grabbed the drink and took a sip, he gave a silly smile after the first sip. "pay the bill and meet us outside, we will wait in the car" Kajal said and we got off our seats. We stepped out of the cafe, and I still wonder why I didn't look back at it. That place still has a ton of good memories. We sat inside the car, and I started tearing up. "Heyyyy did he say something to you? Did he hurt you? Do we need to whoop his ass?" Kajal said, holding on to my shoulder. "I don't know if I made the right choice; I mean, I do still like him, and well, my parents loved each other, and here they are, so basically love fails, but what if this didn't?" She wiped my tears and hugged me; it was a very uncomfortable hug as she was in the driver's seat and I was in the passenger's seat. She held me tight. "Forget him; I'm sad that you are shifting and going so far," she said. "Won't you guys visit me?" I asked. "We definitely will." My heart felt warmth, and this was a different kind of peace. Friendship is always peaceful. I could relate to Anushka's 'pyaar mein junoon hai par dosti mein sukoon hai.' We were on the road, and it was still raining. I felt chills all over my body because I was sitting right in front of the car A/C. It got really silent, as it was my last day in Mumbai; we all were a little emotional. At times like these, I feel sheer frustration. Frustration towards men. And this time it was on my dad; he got a new job as a dean at Pune's 'Pune International College, and our lives were turned upside down. Mom had an interior store that we had to shut down due to the shift. Mom didn't react much to that; I had seen her getting bored in her work; she had stopped putting her love into it long back. My maternal aunts and uncle always told me how much my parents were in love, but I never saw them dancing or loving each other. I've learned about love through movies and stories. And those experiences of falling in love each time the hero stops you at the airport hit different. And those experiences and stories and emotions helped me come to the conclusion that Rahil was not the one. Kajal pulled over the car near my society; she sensed that I wasn't in my best mood. "Don't worry, we will visit you till you are in Pune, and I well even though I don't want you to go, but I will pray that you get admission to the fancy college of paintings," she said looking at me, and we both were kinda frozen for that moment. She picked her sling bag from the side and threw it at Abhishek. "Kitna soyega, she is leaving tomorrow and we didn't even get her anything." "Kal subha you're leaving na, don't worry I promise I will come to see you and get you something special." I gave her a hug and looked outside, it was still raining. I looked at my shoes and prepared myself to step into the rain. I got off the car and waved her.

The main door was open when I entered my apartment, and I was drenched; yes, my shoes got wet too. I took my shoes off before getting in. The living room was packed with cartons piled up on the left. Cupboards and tables were on the right, and a small passage was left for humans to walk. And there, pacing around in stress, was Dad. He was on a call. He looked at me for a couple of seconds and kept talking to the movers; it looked like they were waiting for the rain to stop. I walked to my room as fast as I could because I didn't want to wet the floor. My room looked nothing like it did.

Mom was sitting on a chair there with my suitcase kept on a table in front of her. She was taking out my clothes. She looked up at me and held out my clothes. "How did you know?" She saw us from the window. We lived on the 6th floor, and the entrance to the society was clearly visible from my living room window. "I saw you guys, I knew it tum bheegi hui aaogi." I took the clothes from her hands and went inside my bathroom. I locked the door, and a part of me wanted to turn the shower on and cry underneath it like girls do after a breakup in the movies. But that would just be a waste of time. I took my t-shirt off, which got stuck on my hair and managed to pull a few strands off my scalp. "Ouch." I can still feel that pain. Taking off wet clothes is a task.

I stepped out of the bathroom, and she was still there. I was so lost in my thought that I didn't notice how good she looked. She was wearing a mustard yellow loose-fit kurta with elbow-length sleeves and off-white palazzo pants with all her hair kept beautifully on her right shoulder and a very small bindi. "No mom, not today please," I said, with wide eyes, just to make sure that she knows I'm not in the mood. She always does it, after every fight or breakup of mine she gives me song therapy, where she plays a 70s or 80s Bollywood song that would match my situation. She believed that if you let yourself feel the emotion to its fullest then it makes it easier for you to move on from it. It's like doing justice to your feelings. But the only problem with this was that it worked, every time. And it didn't give me time to be the main character who is in pain. It made me move on easily. "I have a perfect song for you," she started scrolling on her phone screen. "Mommmm, I'm not sad, I am okay and," I said, and I didn't know what was ahead of that and. "And?" she questioned, as she did. She knew everything that goes inside my head. "Nothing," I tossed the towel and sat on the floor next to her chair. "I'm not liking myself right now mom." "Why is that?" she pushed my hair behind my ears, in an assuring way that no matter what she will always like me. I was desperate to tell her everything but I didn't know what was going on inside of me. For the first time there was no excitement in this conversation. "I never loved him, and I still stayed with him, and the minute it got inconvenient for me, I backed off." When those words came out of my mouth, I realized how wrong I was and I messed up with someone. I could feel my face frowning and my throat getting heavier making it difficult to gulp and talk. It felt like I had no control over my own facial expressions. I bowed down, and she held me by my shoulders. My vision got blurry, and tears started falling off. "It's not your fault bachha," she wiped my tears. "I know what you did is not really right, but you can fix it by apologizing and never taking anyone else's feelings for granted." "It's not so easy, I mean I will apologize, but he deserves to be loved, he has loved me so much but I could not give him even a little." "I have a perfect song for you," she said with a smirk on her lips; I knew she wouldn't give up, and well, her tricks work every time. I started laughing with teary eyes.

It rained the whole night. The next morning, as I stepped out of my building thinking about how it's my last day here, we lived in this building for 5 years. I looked ahead of me, and two very familiar faces were looking at me with a smile brighter than the sun. The day was very cloudy. I made a run towards them, and for a couple of seconds, I was confused about whom to hug first; I did a little math so that I would be able to hug them both at the same time. But Kajal stepped forward, Kajal being 3 inches taller than me, wrapped me in her arms. Her bony fingers were pressed against my back and could probably be pierced through. Man, she could be a model. I could smell a strong deodorant and got confused for a second and then a warm body covered mine. It was Abhishek hugging the two of us. A drop straight from the cloud fell on Abhishek's head. "Lagta hai barish hone wali hai." He said.

The three of us burst into laughter. They handed me a small box which was gift-wrapped. I dug my nail into the wrapper to open it. "No not now, open it later, at least not in front of us." "Okayyyy I'm intrigued." I chuckled and kept it in my bag. I turned back to look at mom, but she wasn't there; I looked around the parking lot, and they both were leaning onto our car looking in our direction. The weather was cloudy and breezy. I wanted to cry but didn't want to make the two of them sad. I held Kajal's hand really tightly "promise me you guys will visit." "Yessss hum San Francisco bhi aa jayenge tu bole toh." Abhishek said. I gave them a hug again and walked back towards the car; I kept turning back at them, waving at them over and over.

CHAPTER 2

The journey began, and I was sitting all alone in the back seat, lost in my thoughts. I looked outside the window, and we were yet to touch the highway. The roads were not that jammed as we left early in the morning, but there were high chances of rain. The weather was beautiful and windy, and the smell of wet mud always intoxicated me. It reminded me of Rahil.

I looked at my Dad, who was focused on driving and didn't care to look at my mom. Although my dad was extremely good-looking at the age of 50, I could imagine what a heartthrob he would be in his 20s. But my mom, she still looked amazing, and if I were in his place, I would have cherished every moment with my mom.

I took my phone out of my handbag, glancing at the wrapped gift Kajal and Abhishek had given me, which brought a smile to my face. I didn't touch it as I planned on opening it only after entering my new house.

I took out my earphones and connected them to my phone. I played a romantic Bollywood song, and on cue, the clouds rumbled. I rolled down my windows. I looked at my phone again, hoping there would be a text from Rahil, but he had not messaged me. There was a time when he could not stay without texting me for even 20 minutes, and now he didn't text or call for more than 24 hours. I felt emotional, but I knew it was for the best.

I could feel my eyes getting heavier as I hadn't slept properly last night. I was excited, nervous, and sad. Excited for the new place and sad for breaking up with Rahil. I had fallen asleep with the windows down and woke up an hour later when raindrops hit my forehead.

"Where are we?" I asked, struggling to put my hair behind my ears as they were tangled into a big knot. I had fallen asleep with my hair open, expecting to wake up with it floating in the air like in the movies.

"We are 1 hour and 10 minutes away from the location. Do you wanna eat something?" mom asked I rolled up the window and took a hairbrush out of my bag, trying to untangle my hair.

"Um, yeah, I am a little hungry, and I also need to pee," I said to mom.

"Zaid, can we stop at some dhaba or some restaurant?" mom asked dad.

"Yeah, there's one on our way, 10 minutes away," Dad said. I checked, pushing my bladder a little to see if I could hold my pee in for the next 10 minutes.

"Yeah, can wait for the next 10 minutes," I said, focusing on my hair.

Ten minutes later, we stopped at a food joint. It looked like an eat street with all the famous fast food joints in one place. I got out of the car and walked towards the sign that said 'washroom.' I peed and got out of the booth; my life felt like it was running on autopilot mode. I looked at my reflection in the stained mirror of that ugly bathroom. I looked fine.

I came out and saw mom and dad eating Vada Pav. There was one kept aside for me too. I had not eaten anything since morning, and I checked the time. It was 12 pm, and after looking at the time, my hunger increased. I took a big bite of the Vada Pav and looked around. I saw a guy looking at me; I immediately covered my face with my hand and swallowed the food.

I looked again at his direction, but the guy was gone. "Ugh, God, my life has become so boring. What would it take for you to add some drama..." I mumbled.

"What are you saying?" Dad asked. I took another big bite. "Nothing, I'm just bored, and I miss my friends," I said.

We got back into the car, and I plugged in my earphones, ready to get lost in the beautiful view and my songs. After an hour, we entered the society. I looked outside, and the place looked beautiful. We entered a housing society. I've lived in apartments all my life; I've never had a whole house to myself. Those houses were really pretty.

My mom was saying something to dad, and he smiled and said something back to her. I couldn't hear because I was blasting my ears with music. I took one of the earphones off; I wanted to know what they were talking about because they were smiling. This new place was already working.

'Hum Bane Tum Bane Ek Duje Ke Liye' was playing on the radio. "Sing naaaa," my mom pressed my dad's shoulder, trying to convince him to sing the line.

"I don't know what you say," dad literally said those lines instead of singing. I'm a sucker for such moments. I smiled and looked outside.

Dad pulled over near a two-story bungalow; it had a balcony with glass railings and a young man standing on that balcony facing towards the house. He was wearing a faded olive green tee. He had massive shoulders, and every muscle of his arm moved every time he took his hands near his face. Although only the back of his head was visible, I guessed the man was smoking.

I got out of the car, a little mesmerized by the guy. I kept looking at him. "This is not our house, Ahilya, this one is." Dad pointed at a house right behind me. I turned my head, and there was my house. It looked very similar to the house with the hot guy. I pulled my handbag out of the car, pretending to look for something in it while looking at dad. I just wanted his eyes off me so that I could turn back real quick and get a glimpse of him again. I kinda wanted him to notice me too.

Mom was already inside the front yard, walking towards the main door of the house. "Hurry up."

"Yeah, I just can't find my earphones."

"They are in your ears, Ahilya." The tone got really sarcastic. "Oh yeah." I acted silly. It always works. He started moving further, and I quickly turned my head. He was gone; the hot guy was no longer standing there. I sulked and followed dad inside.

I didn't even notice the yard; I just walked inside. It was a huge house, especially for someone who lived in Mumbai.

As we entered, there was a huge living room on the left, a little passage joining the kitchen and the staircase on the right. There were no rooms downstairs.

Mom was already on the top floor, and I realized that there's a room up there with a balcony. My hot neighbor has a room with a balcony. Could this be the beginning of a new love story? "Possibly," I said that out loud.

"What possibly?" Dad asked.

"Just singing the song I'm listening to, possibly you are the one lalalala." I made up a song.

He kept looking at me so intensely I felt he could read my thoughts for a second. Even Mom has told me in the past that Dad could read her thoughts.

I forced a smile on my face and ran up to Mom and to the room with a balcony. I climbed the last three stairs and could literally hear my heart pounding. I realized that I was not that fit. But that realization didn't break my heart. What broke my heart was... Newsflash, my house had a public balcony. The balcony was in the hall. It was not in any room, and that sucked.

I picked a room right next to it. I looked around, and there were three rooms. 2 at the back and 1 next to the balcony. The best part was that the other two rooms were at the back. "Can work with this balcony too."

"Why don't you take the room next to ours, Aalu?" Mom came up with this great idea.

"Mom, I really like this room, and it's also next to the balcony, and you know back in Mumbai how badly I wanted one." Mom was very easy to convince. She smirked at me. I don't know about Dad, but Mom, she could definitely read me like a book.

I checked my room, and well, it was way smaller than I expected. I opened the balcony and stepped out. It definitely needed some cleaning. I peeped down; our truck just pulled in.

I looked ahead at the 'hot guy's' balcony. His room had a sliding French window. So did ours.

I could see very thick blue velvet curtains hanging through the open window. His bed was visible too. A cream-colored quilt lay half on the bed and half on the floor. The floor was completely carpeted. And the lights were off. A leg pushed the quilt completely off the bed. He was on his bed, and all I could see was his leg. I couldn't see the details, like if the leg was shaved or hairy. It looked almost hairy to me.

A loud thud noise interrupted my stalking. Maybe that was a sign from God. I ignored. I turned towards the noise; the movers were taking the bed into my room.

"Madam, yeh bed kaha lagana hai?" a worker who had come from the packers and movers company asked, but my eyes were stuck on that leg.

I looked at the worker and pointed towards my new bedroom.

For the next 30 minutes, he and his other mates kept filling my room. My paintings, my cabinets, my dreamcatchers, my books.

"Madam, sab rakh diya hai aap dekh lo." I smiled at him just to be polite, though I wanted him to just leave. How mean Ahilya! How mean...

They left my room and started with my parents' room. I entered my room and looked at a painting of a couple sitting on Marine Drive, which was inspired by Kajal and Abhishek.

Which reminded me of the gift that they had given to me.

I opened my bag and pulled out the gift box. I unwrapped it, and there was a beautiful red box.

I opened that box, and there was a glass keychain that had a picture of 'Radha Krishna' made with gold inside of it.

Even though I didn't believe in God, I loved, loved, loved the gift.

I took my phone and called them instantly. Kajal picked. "It was Abhishek's choice."

"It's beautiful." "Don't cry on it now. I will call you later; we are at his place and no one's home." She literally yelled out those last words; I could picture him pulling her. These guys are really adorable.

She hung up the phone, and it was quiet again. I looked around, and my room was a mess.

I started doing mental math on how I will design this room.

I had at least 7 paintings. I looked at the couple's picture again and placed it right in front of my bed. Then next to my bed was the painting I drew when I saw a waterfall for the first time in my life.

That was my happy place, in 2016 when my parents took me to Kerala.

And the other paintings were not so important, so I just kept them aside, just in case Mom wanted to hang them around the house.

After around 4 hours of cleaning and setting, my room was half done. I had totally forgotten about the guy. When I stepped outside the room, it was pitch dark. I turned the lights on. The hall was already set. The TV was on the wall, our couch was placed in front of the TV. It was clean.

I walked to my parents' room to find my dad was fast asleep, and I could hear the pitter-patter of water coming from inside the bathroom.

I assumed Mom was taking a shower. I walked quietly to the bathroom door and knocked.

"Mom, should I order food?" I asked.

"Don't call for pizza." "Fine, I'll order Subway." "Done," we both loved Subway salads and we could literally eat them all day.

I went out to the hall and pulled a mat from one of the cartons. I took it outside and sat on the balcony. This time it was not for the boy; this time it was for the new place, the wide sky, and the couple of visible stars, and mainly it was for the moon.

Yes, I am and was a lover of the moon. The reason was very simple. The moon is that place which you can see and love but from afar. It's something you can never reach.

It loves you back too; if it didn't, it wouldn't be coming back every night to meet you.

It teases you, loves you, and inspires you but from afar. I kept staring at the moon; I looked at my neighbor's balcony, and the glass door was shut. I looked down and saw a shadow in his yard. There he was, in a black shirt, opening his main gate, probably to take his car out.

I could see his face. He had a long face, a sharp jawline, dark eyebrows, dark brown hair.

And that shirt... that shirt could kill.

He had his first 2 buttons undone as if he was giving away a teaser of a really hot movie.

He looked up at me, and I froze. I wanted to look away, but for some reason, I just couldn't.

I don't know if I froze or the time froze. All I remember is that we were looking at each other without even blinking, and for a second, every possibility flashed in front of my eyes.

Trust me, a lot of that got true.

And he looked away. Why would he do that? Why would he look away? We were having our moment, or maybe it was not his as much as it was mine.

He sat inside the car, and he looked at me again. My eyes were never this shameless. They didn't want to look away.

I was weirdly attracted to his arms. He held the steering wheel and started his car. He drove it out of his yard and stopped. He got out of the car, and my heart stopped. Like he would walk to me, and he would say something. He didn't; he got down to close the gates behind him.

I could see his forearm veins, and I looked at his face again; his eyes were on me.

He walked around his car till the door, and his eyes did stay on me. I wish I had it in me to pinch myself and check if I wasn't hallucinating. He opened the door and got in his car. I didn't move.

My senses were so amplified that I could imagine how he smelled.

He sat still for a good 3 seconds before driving away. He didn't look at my direction though, but after the moment ended, I was left confused. What had just happened?

Was I attracted to him because I needed a rebound, or was it something different? I was no longer thinking about Rahil.

But the thought that I was not thinking about Rahil actually made me think of him. I picked up my phone, which was switched off.

I turned it on. For a few seconds, there was nothing, and after those few seconds, a wave of notifications attacked my phone. A few Instagram notifications and a few texts from Kajal.

Did you reach?

Why is your phone off?

How's the new place?

I kinda forgot to tell her. It was a shocker for me. How could I forget to call her? Is this how people forget their best friends? I dialed her number that instance

"What's up, bitch, you already forgot about us, huh?" I laughed, after a whole day of work and cleaning and a little fun, I finally felt home.

The saying is very true that home is actually a feeling.

"I have sooooo much to tell you."

"Arrey, abhi toh gayi hai, abhi se jaadu chala diya?"

"Nooo, nothing like that." my jaw started hurting because of the super-wide smile I had on my face.

"Goo onnnn.. " "I have a hot neighbor. Aaaaa"

"Aaaaaaaaaaaaaaokayyyyyy." we both were screaming in excitement. "Okay and what's his name." "Ek hi din hua hai, give me some time yaa" "Cool girl maze kar."

"Chal I'll call you later and I'll keep you updated." I was still smiling looking at his balcony again. Isn't it exciting when your friends are equally happy for you?

Throughout dinner, mom kept giving me a weird look.

I was going to tell her about this new guy but not yet. But I knew that she already knew.

We did the dishes together, and before she could say anything, I said, "let's go for a walk after this is done?"

"Hmm," she just shook her head with a smile.

We stepped out, and the air was so soothing, the moon looked very pretty, and the place looked gorgeous. I was honestly no longer mad at dad for making us shift here.

We started walking. "Handsome toh hai." Mom said.

"Mom! Who?" "His dad" mom and her sarcasm. We shared a look, and we kept walking.

"I would suggest taking some time before you get into things beta. You've just got out of a relationship, and you did hurt another person because you were not sure about him when you got into the relationship."

"I know mom, and I promise I won't rush into things; I won't get into a relationship till I'm very sure that I love him."

"Ohh matlab you want to try it yeh final hai?"

"Yaar mumma." I started walking backward. I wanted to see her face and look into her eyes when I told her this. Her phone beeped, and it was a text from dad; she started reading it while I was still speaking.

"I'm telling you it's not a rebound, and it's just a crush; I'm just healing by looking at him." and bang I bumped into someone.

My nose liked the person behind me already. I turned back, and it was that black shirt; his chest was right at my eye level, and I looked up. Yes, it was him.

He was taller than I expected, and that face. He looked at me, and his mouth opened a bit.

"I'm sorry." I said.

He squinched his eyes and walked away; my heart, my body, my brain worked as a team and took a break. They practically stopped.

I looked at mom, and she looked impressed. "hot toh hai" she said looking at me, and he turned.

"You said something?" he asked. Mom's eyes widened up "no nothing," I said, and even though it was written all over his face that he didn't buy it, he turned and kept walking.

"Did you notice something?" mom held my hand and pulled it toward her like she's going to break a news to me, but she got to whisper it.

"What?" "He went in a car and came back walking."

I took a pause. The whole car moment came flashing in front of my eyes, but how did she know? Was the question that hit my brain like a truck?

Is she a wizard?

"How do you know he went in a car?' "I came out of the shower, I went down to turn on the light of the living room and the yard, and that's when I saw him looking at our balcony, and I knew that you were sitting on the balcony. Simple math beta simple math." She is a wizard.

"Wowwww if you were one of those strict mothers I would be dead by now." She lowered her chin and looked at me with suspicious eyes and a smile, just to tease me.

CHAPTER 3

Shraddha

I received a text on my phone, and I looked up at it. It was from Zaid. It was a forwarded message.

Zaid: Welcome you to the society Mr. Mirza. Hope to see you tomorrow at 7 am at the society park. - Ravi (Society secretary)

Zaid couldn't go to the meeting as he had to go to work, and hence he had asked me to go in his place.

Shrad: What is this about?

Zaid: Just a meet and greet.

Shrad: Okay, I'll go.

The next morning, I opened my eyes. I looked at the other side of the bed, and Zaid was already in the shower. My back was a little sore as I had exhausted myself yesterday. I got up and tied my hair in a bun. I walked down to the kitchen to make tea for the two of us.

I turned on the stove and placed the boiler on it. I added the tea into it and waited for it to boil. My body worked on autopilot mode in the morning. My routine had been the same for 25 years.

I added milk and sugar and waited for it to boil together. I added cardamom and ginger into it and waited for another minute.

I took out two cups from the top right shelf and poured the tea into the two cups.

I took them out to the dining table and waited for Zaid to come down.

He came down instantly, "Good morning!" he said and sat next to me.

"Good morning," I replied. He picked up the cup and took a sip. "Perfect!" he said and smiled at me. "Excited for the first day?" I asked.

"I don't know, I don't feel excitement," he said. I felt sad for him. I kept looking at him and took a sip.

We didn't say anything to each other till he finished his tea. He stood up and picked his bag.

I walked up to him, and we hugged. The hug was a mere formality. It had been a formality for the last 20 years. He walked out of the house, and I followed him. He sat inside his car, and I waved at him.

I looked at the time, and it was 6 am. I went up and got ready for the meeting. I had learned to put up a smile and keep myself together for my daughter, but today I was losing myself.

I was under the shower when my eyes gave up. I broke into tears and tried to calm myself down. It was never Zaid's fault that we were no longer in love with each other. Maybe it was mine.

I got dressed and walked out of my house. The weather was a little chilly. I walked towards the park where the meeting was going to take place. There was a wooden hood in the middle of the park around which they had chairs.

I saw a man from afar, sitting on one of the chairs. The man looked at me and almost got up off his chair. I looked away, and he sat back on it. I went towards the chair and picked the one far away from him.

No one came in for the next 10 minutes, and we kept looking at each other occasionally. Every time our eyes met, my gut felt weird, like my heart was playing tennis inside. My lungs would fill a little extra.

Slowly, the place started filling up, and I left my chair to go and greet everyone. A group of women entered together, covered in shawls. They looked at me and smiled but didn't stop to talk. I felt awkward and looked towards the man again.

This time he got up from his chair and started walking towards me. I looked away as my heart stopped. I followed the group of those women, trying to catch up with their pace and avoid the man. I stopped them and said, "Hello, I'm Shraddha, we just shifted here."

"oh hi, you're Shraddha? Mr. Mirza's wife?" a lady asked, stressing on my Hindu name with my husband's Muslim surname. I was taken aback a little by their question.

"yes, I am his wife." I replied; the woman looked at me weirdly.

"please have a seat." She gave me a weird smile and showed me the seating area. I knew that people would be talking about me now; they know my name which does not match my surname.

"Hello," a deep voice greeted me from behind. I turned to look, and it was the same man. I had to take a deep breath to be able to feel normal. I smiled at him and held my hand out. I would have to agree that the man looked fit for his age.

"HI, I'm Shraddha!" I said shaking his hand.

"Hi, I'm Yash." He said; I was mesmerized for a couple of seconds, but I had to stop myself. I looked around, and the women who ignored me were now staring at me without even blinking.

Yash was a handsome man; he looked like he was in his mid-50s but had been maintaining himself. He had a salt and pepper look and a very deep voice.

He led the way to the sitting areas and pulled a chair for me to sit next to him. It felt like my blood got warmer in my veins, and I felt comfortable.

"So Mr. Mirza couldn't make it?" he asked.

"He had to reach the university by 7:30," I looked at my watch, "he must be there by now."

"I didn't know he was a college student, what is he studying?" he looked into my eyes with curiosity.

I laughed at that joke of his, and he didn't look away for some reason. I noticed that and stopped laughing. The way he looked at me made me feel seen but generated feelings which were long gone.

"What do you do?" I asked him, not because I was interested to know but to distract him.

"Oh, I am a doctor, and a father and that's it."

"Not a husband?" I asked.

"No, I'm not a husband, sorry for the disappointment ma'am."

"Oh, I'm so sorry; you must miss her a lot?"

"Ohh no no no she is alive, we are just divorced." I covered my mouth in disbelief that I guessed it so wrong, and we both laughed again. Without noticing that people were eyeing us.

"So I have one daughter." I said.

"I have one son." He continued.

"Oh wow, how old is he?"

"He is 23 right now, his name is Yohanne, and he wishes to elope soon," he said with a sarcastic smile.

"Hmmm interesting, she is 20, her name is Ahilya, and she is also planning to leave soon." I said. I wanted him to speak more; I was enjoying the conversation even though it wasn't the most interesting conversation.

"Kids these days, they just wanna leave and start living..." he said and looked away.

"Are you getting emotional?" I asked and tried to take a look at his eyes.

"Not really, I mean I got Yohanne when he was like 7 years old, and since then he has been my whole world." He said.

"You got Yohanne as in?" I asked.

"As in, I got Yohanne's custody from his mom when he was 7," he replied. I had so many questions, but I decided to keep them to myself. I looked at his eyes; he had pain in them but also wisdom. He looked at me looking at his eyes. I didn't feel the need to look away. I kept looking at him.

"Mrs. Mirza?" a loud voice on the microphone announced my name; we both shook for a split second and looked ahead at the direction. The meeting had begun long back, and we were just lost. I looked at him again in embarrassment, and he blushed.

I got up from my seat and smiled at everyone, I joined my hands to greet everyone. "Namaste, I'm Shraddha Mirza, and I'm so glad to be welcomed in this beautiful society." I bowed and stood there waiting for a response. I didn't know what else we're supposed to say at such occasions.

I avoided looking at Yash, but I could sense his eyes were on me. "Thank you, Mrs. Mirza; we hope to see Mr. Mirza soon," the secretary said smiling at me. I looked around, and the women were looking at me like I had stolen something.

I took a deep breath and decided to avoid those looks. I sat on my seat, and my knee touched Yash's knee. My heart stopped, and my blood got warm. I didn't move my knee, and he kept it still too. There was something about that subtle touch. The touch that says I feel you, I see you, and I'm here. Who was he to even give me those feelings? I didn't look at him for the rest of the meeting, and I didn't even move my leg. He did move a bit, but he would end up touching his knee to mine.

I closed my eyes, "What's happening to you?" I asked myself and opened my eyes and saw everyone getting up. The meeting was over, and I looked at my right, and Yash wasn't there. I looked ahead, and he was talking to a lady. I notice that the lady was smiling way too much; he was advising her on something, I couldn't hear clearly. His arms moved as he explained. He turned to look at me, while talking to that woman, he saw me staring at him again.

I smiled this time, and he smiled back. I got up from my seat and started walking towards my house. I walked past him, and I could hear what he was saying. "I'll see you at the clinic... yeah bye." He said and left the conversation. I kept walking at my pace. He followed and did a little sprint to reach me.

"Our conversation was interrupted ma'am," he said from behind. I turned back and smiled. I continued walking. A little slower this time. "I forgot what we were talking about," I said; I did try to remember but I couldn't.

"Umm, we were talking about being friends," he said, I stopped walking, I looked at him, and raised my eyebrows. "Umm, you are very direct," I said. I was shocked.

"What do you mean?" he asked.

"I just mean that I don't feel like this is the age where a good man like you would ask a married woman like me to be his friend," I explained.

He kept walking with me.

"And why not?" he asked.

"I don't know, it just feels inappropriate," I said.

"Hmmm." He said and continued walking with me. "Are you going to drop me home and then go back?" I asked and looked at him; he turned to me and smiled.

"As you wish," he said. I was confused as he was the one walking with me and following me. We reached my house, and I stopped a few meters before. I showed him the house and said, "This is me, now you can go back." He smiled and looked down with his fingers on his lips.

He started laughing the next second. I had not seen a man laughing like that; I stood there confused, but seeing this complete stranger laugh made me happy too. "Why are you laughing like a kid?" I asked and almost chuckled myself.

"You assumed I was following you to drop you?" he asked.

"Were you not?" I asked him back.

"Umm, it's an honest mistake, I live right here, in front of your house," he said pointing at the house where my daughter's crush lived.

"Ohhhh.. oh my god. Okay.." I mumbled.

"It's okay Shraddha, take care, I'll see you around," he said and turned towards his house.

"Yash!" I called him. He turned back and waited for me to speak. "What's the name of your son again?" I asked.

"Yohhane."

CHAPTER 4

Ahilya

I was sitting on my bed looking at my phone when mom entered; the moment I laid eyes on her, I assumed something bad had happened, and she had to run to give me the bad news. I removed the blankets off me to get down. I started calculating and assuming every possibility there could be like: Did someone die? From her family? Did my dad get my grandfather's money? Did someone have a heart attack at the meeting? Did she get a job? All these questions, and what came out of my mouth was, "Kya hua?" ("What happened?").

"Yohanne Sharma." Two words, who could this be? You know when you are in an exam hall trying to think of an answer and nothing hits your brain. And you doubt your capabilities. Well, such situations will make you believe otherwise. It took my brain 1 second to guess who Yohhane Sharma could be.we both were standing in front of each other extremely still, almost in a creepy way with eyes wide opened.

"The hot guy?" I asked. "Was he there? Did he introduce himself to you?" I started shooting questions at her before she could even speak. "No, his dad was there." She replied. "Ohh, his dad must be hot too," I said. "You bet. But not as hot as your dad," she replied. "Yeah yeah, sure," I said with the utmost sarcasm. She rolled her eyes.

"Now will you find him, or I'll have to do it for you too?" she said. She can be savage at times, though.

At times like those, I felt really lucky to have a mother like her. I knew her so well, but I didn't know my dad. I was happy because of the way she was, I was sad because I somewhere felt that she didn't deserve that. She deserved to be loved and cherished. I always wanted to be like her. Maybe I will, who knows.

She gave me a quick yet tight hug and got up; she looked out the window. There was a window next to my bed, and guess what. We could see the Sharma mansion from there. No, it wasn't a mansion, but we just call it that.

I caught her looking out, and she caught my eyes. "Whatt?" "Not as hot as dad ha?" "Shutupp alloo, I love your dad." She blushed a little and brought her hand near to my nose, squeezing it. "Oouchh don't do that, mom." "Then you stop making stories in your head, I mean make your own, mine is done." She smiled at me gracefully and walked out of my room.

Yes, she was looking outside, yes, she wanted to see him. Why? Even though she didn't know. Is it possible to fall in love like that?

Mom left the room and gave me the name I desperately wanted. There was a mirror right in front of my bed, a full-sized mirror; I could see my reflection in it. I didn't look great as my hair was all messy. I walked up to that mirror and said, "Yohanne Sharma ... Ahilya

Sharma ... Ahilya Mirza Sharma?" I had to check if I wanna accept his surname or be feminist and stick to mine. I giggled and covered my face with my hands. Yes, I never felt like that before. I never felt that with Rahil.

I turned around and jumped on the bed. I grabbed my phone, opened Instagram, and typed Y O H A N N E S H A R M A. A long list of men appeared on the screen. It was easy cause he was hot; I could just see the profile pictures of those men and skip. Finally, while scrolling, I came across this account where the man in the profile picture was wearing a black shirt with a glass of beer in his hand. I recognized the shirt. I clicked on the account, and NEWS FLASHHHH the account was private. He had seen me the other day while walking. If I sent him a request, he would know that I'm stalking him. But he didn't know my best friend and what are best friends for if not to let you use their account to stalk your crushh.

I dialed Kajal that instant. "I need your Insta id." "I'll give you, but why?" Yes, we don't do hi, how are you, what's up. This is the sign of true friendship where you just call and come to the point. "The hot guy's account is private." "Abhishake with the capital A." "That's your password?" "Yess, don't judge, just do whatever you want." "Cool love you byeee." "Love you too, keep me updated." I hung up the call and opened her account. 207 DM requests. 18 unread texts. I had to ignore the fact that my bestie is a diva, and the hot guy could possibly fall for her.

I sent him a follow request... and my next step? Wait. I waited for eternity. The wait is the worst part, but these waiting stages are much better than the talking stages. There are multiple possibilities your heart can imagine.

I looked at the time, and it was 8:18 am; I had an urge to stalk his room from my balcony. I got off my bed and started searching my bag like a maniac. I was looking for my hairbrush and my makeup. Well, of course, I wasn't planning to put on any makeup, but I needed my lips to look pink-ish. I looked at my face, and it was oily, and my lips were very dry.

I walked out my room yelling, "Moooommyyyyyyy." "Kyaa huaaaa." "Mere makeup wala bag kaha hai." "Check in your bathroom." "Okayy." I walked down the stairs to the kitchen; she was there cooking something. "Kya bana rahe ho?" "Poha." "Arrey yaar." I grabbed a bottle of water from the fridge and drank straight from the bottle. "What arrey yaar, you never help me with anything and when I make something you throw hazar tantrums." I kept the bottle back and ran back up to my room.

I opened my bathroom door, and my makeup purse was right there; I took my hairbrush out and brushed my hair. I threw the brush next to the washbasin and I pulled my lipstick. I applied it and gave a kiss to my reflection. I walked out to the balcony and started looking at his balcony; I couldn't see his feet from the edge of his bed, which meant he was up. "Tring tring" I heard a bell from below. I looked down and couldn't believe my eyes. He was in a sports attire coming out of his house with his cycle. He looked up at me again, and this time, I was prepared. I looked away. My hair acted perfect by flying over my face, and I was looking at the sky to look mysterious. I turned my head towards him again, and he was gone. Like he missed such a beautiful sight of me being the main character. I could see him going further on his cycle.

I walked back inside and threw myself on the couch. I didn't realize that our TV was fixed on the wall. I tried to turn it on and to my shock, it did turn on. I was going through channels and I stopped at a music channel. I heard my mom's footsteps. And instantly, I knew that she was getting breakfast. And if I didn't run and snatch it from her, by snatching I mean help, if I didn't help her. Then she would start lecturing me on how irresponsible I am. So, I ran. I met her mid stairs and took the plates from her. "Next song me and the hot guy." Me and mom had this game where we would start a music channel on TV and predict something. For instance, the next song would predict how a certain person feels for me. "You mean Yohanne?" "Yess." We settled on the couch with our plates. The ongoing song came to an end, and advertisements started. We were disappointed as advertisements meant no future. "We will be optimistic." Mom took the remote and changed the channel. "Jiss roz se dekha hai unko hum shama jalana bhul gaye" song was going on, and we both screamed and started laughing. We started singing along the song, "Mere saamne waali khidki pe ek chaand ka tukda rehta hai."

An hour went by listening to old Bollywood songs. My head was laid on my mom's lap when I opened my eyes; she was asleep too, and some commercials were coming on the TV. I lowered the volume and looked at the time on my phone; it was 10:05 am. I kept looking at mom, and I wasn't thinking about anything; my brain was blank. She opened her eyes and rubbed her face with her hands. "We slept!" "Yeahh!" "Mom, can I ask for something?" "Sure." She smiled at me and placed her hand on my shoulder. "Can I get a cycle? You know I don't know anyone, and it would be great if I could go cycling in the mornings." I knew that she could see through all my lame explanations, but it was my duty to give one.

"Yess I'll ask dad; you guys can go and pick one tomorrow." "No need for that, mom, I can order it online, and it will come by tomorrow, kardu? Order?" "Okay, do it." I ordered the bicycle, imagining him teaching me how to ride, ill fall and then he will come and pick me up.

That evening I got a notification, and by that time, I had completely forgotten about the request.

I saw that Yohhane Sharma had accepted my follow request. I took a moment to breathe and clicked on his profile to see his pictures. "What a waste." There were just 3 pictures; one was his picture with his cycle where his back was facing the camera. The second picture was a group picture. I looked at the girls in the picture; there were three. One of them was extremely hot. I clicked on the picture to check if she was tagged. She wasn't. The last picture he posted was his profile picture.

I got another notification, and this time it was a text from him.

Yoh: Hey

Kajal: Hey

I texted back, and then I instantly regretted texting that fast.

Yoh: Kajal! Looks like you have a boyfriend already. So why did you send me a request?

Kajal: Yeah, I do, but I don't really love him.

Yes, I regretted saying that too. What the heck was I doing?

Yoh: Okay, so what do you expect from me?

Kajal: Um, nothing.

Yoh: You just wanna follow me? I mean, we might as well cheat on your bf together.

Kajal: Umm, I live in Mumbai, so we can't do that.

I so wanted to kill him; such a playboy he turned out to be. I was about to send him a text telling him what an asshole he is, but his account got blocked from Kajal's end. I sighed and dialed her to say sorry.

Her number was busy; I hung it up from my end and threw the phone next to me on the bed. My phone started to ring, and it was Kajal. I picked it up, and the voices from the other side were just too chaotic. "Hey, why are you yelling?" It was a conference call between me, Kajal, and Abhishek. "Tell him that it was you, Aalu," Kajal said furiously; her words pierced my ears. "Abhishek calm down, man." "What do you mean by calm down? She is cheating on me, and you are supporting her?" "She is not; it was my fault, I wanted to see that guy, he is from Pune, he is my neighbor." "Oh, and you want me to believe you?" "Yes, tomorrow morning the first thing I'll do is click a picture of him and send you?" "Fine, till then I'm not talking to the both of you." He hung up. "Kajal? Are you good?" "No yaar Ahalya, wtf was that?" "Chill, ill fix it." "Ill talk to you later Al." "Hmm, take care." I felt like crap for creating a mess in their life and for what? For a playboy like him. I needed to click his picture, and that can be done when he goes cycling.

The next morning, I got up and decided to talk to him; I was his new neighbor, and I could totally do that, so what if he had a hot girlfriend or he was a playboy. I got dressed up; I wore black yoga pants and a gray tee with a high ponytail. I had my phone, and at 9 am, I walked out. It was a sunny day in a rainy season. I smiled looking at the sky, I was excited and felt confident. I was walking near the house so that I don't miss him. My plan was to say hi to him, and when he stops, I would just start a random conversation and take a video real quick.

I looked at the time and knew it could take him more 3-4 minutes to come out. I started looking around the society I could see mountains from afar, beautiful greenery around, it wasn't as humid as Mumbai. The wind blew, and I knew that he had just stepped out of his house. I turned and saw him walking out of his house with his cycle. He was wearing a black sports tee with black cycling shorts with a little helmet. He hopped on his cycle, and I could not just stand right there looking at him. So I pretended to tie my shoelaces. His cycle came closer to me; I noticed his forearms; they had really less to no hair on them. "Ha hey hi" I fumbled. He just passed by riding his cycle and completely ignoring me. I felt humiliated to my bones, and I just turned and walked inside my house.

The next day...

TINNGGGINGG... Our doorbell rang; mom was in the bathroom, so I had to take it. I opened the door, and it was the cycle that I ordered. I jumped in excitement. "Maam OTP" the delivery guy asked

"2214" I said and took the cycle. I unwrapped it, and I wanted to try it out that very instant. I wasn't in my sports attire and I didn't even realise in my excitement what time it was. I took the cycle outside, and I sat on it. "Woah" I lost my balance for a bit.

"Give it another try" I said to myself and gave it another try, and I could go on for like 2 seconds and lost control again. I looked ahead and then at the handles of the cycle. "We have to do it." I started paddling; I almost got it, and then again, I lost my balance, and this time, I fell. "Ouch" I fell over my left shoulder and scratched my elbow. I started blowing air on my wound when a hand came over my shoulder. "You good?" I turned around to see whom this hand belonged to. Halfway through, I understood it was Yohanne. I looked at his face; it was covered with sweat. His cycle was on its stand right next to him. He looked so hot. My ears suddenly decided to go deaf, and all I could hear was my heartbeat and all that happened in 5 seconds. For some reason, I didn't take his hand; I got up on my own, left my cycle there, and ran into my house. I got inside and felt embarrassed for what I just did to him. I looked through the side glass of our main door. He took my cycle and parked it inside my front yard. "Can I undo what I just did, god?" "Wtf Ahalya Mirza, what the literal heck. Why would you run on him like that? Look at him; he is so sweet; he can't be a playboy." I stomped my feet on the floor and saw him walking to his house. "Ahhhhh" I cried and as I turned, my mom was standing right there, she was stunned. She was staring at me with super wide eyes. "Ahalya, are you possessed?" "No mom, I'm dumb."

CHAPTER 5

Yohanne

Yoh: So tomorrow at 7 am? Al: Yeah, see you tomorrow...

3 days back

When I got back to my senses, I was standing in front of the mirror wearing a black shirt. The room was extremely cold; I looked to my left at the AC, it was 17°. I took a deep breath; my hands didn't feel like they were a part of my body until I moved them closer to my face. I touched my face. "What did I smoke?" I asked myself. My face was wet with sweat, and my skin was cold. My shirt was half unbuttoned. I started buttoning it up. My vision felt a little blurred; I tried focusing on the wallpaper on my walls. I could see the details of the bluish-gray wallpaper in my room; it had very little white flowers which I had never noticed before. The yellow light was on yet everything was so gray, from my wallpaper to my bedsheet. Something buzzed on the dresser. My phone was kept there. It was moving slowly on its own. The screen was flashing a name, 'Sumair'. Triinngggggg, it felt like a muselet popped open from my ears. I could hear the phone ring suddenly. I looked back in the mirror, and I was perspiring heavily. I could see things normally and could feel my tongue again. I took a few tissues from the tissue box kept on my dresser. I wiped my face and took a deep breath again. I grabbed my phone and walked out of my room. I had to cross the hall to reach the kitchen. A man was sitting on the couch; no matter how hard I wanted to ignore his existence, he would show up. "Will you be home for dinner?" he asked

I didn't answer; I kept walking. I entered the kitchen and pulled the fridge door. There were just 2 bottles of water; I took one and chugged on it. I had to stop to catch my breath. There was a horizontally wide sliding glass window, through which I could see the road and the house in front of ours, very clearly. There was a girl on the balcony. Her hair was open, and I could barely see her face. I got the bottle near my mouth and took another big sip of it. I could feel the cold water flowing through my intestine.

I kept the bottle on the kitchen platform and left. I walked out of my house, and she was still there; I opened the main gate and got her attention. I took a second to look at her; time stopped; she looked back at me. I stood there for a second. I saw her eyes, not clearly, but they looked beautiful from afar. Her lips looked soft and a little red. I wasn't feeling anything as such; in fact, it had been years since I felt anything, but there was a sense of warmth I felt while looking at her. My phone buzzed, and I knew I had to leave. I got into my car and got it out; I got down from the car to close the main gate. I looked at her again, and she stood still. I closed the door and came back in my car. I started the car and left her standing there. As soon as my car entered the road I forgot about her. I was going to a club with my friends; my phone was buzzing constantly. I didn't really like going out with them a lot, but once or twice a month wasn't that undoable. This was the toughest time for me because my mind was on the loose. There weren't any distractions, which allowed my mind to think whatever it wanted. I switched on the radio hoping it would help. The words were hitting my ears indeed, but nothing was getting decoded. Men don't cry, right? So how could I? At least now I'm capable enough to keep it all in. But what would I do about these thoughts? The scene flashed in front of my eyes. When I was forcefully brought to India and I had to go to school and study, I would usually break into tears missing my mom and how every other guy in my class showed how tough they were by beating me up. And the man who just asked if I will be having dinner with him, never trusted me, never took my side. I became what the world wanted me to be. I pulled in at the parking lot of the club and dialed Sumair; he was my only hope, my only friend in this selfish world. I laid my head on the seat and waited for him to pick up the call. "Hello kaha hai bhai?" he asks from the other side of the call. "Gadi mein hu bro, I don't feel like coming in. I'm going back; I'll just smoke a J and sleep" "Don't ditch us; I'm coming to get you, and agar tu wanha se hila then you're dead." He said

"I'll leave soon but"

"Done, main hee drop karunga." He said and I sighed and kept my phone aside. I looked in the rearview mirror; my face didn't have any expression on, and the jaw felt super stiff. I opened my mouth wide to stretch my locked jaw. There was a couple standing a couple of feet away from my car; the girl was leaning on to another car, and the boy was yelling at her. My windows were closed, and still, I could hear a muffled sound of his words. The girl kept looking down; she didn't even look up at him. I wondered what she must have done for him to treat her that way. A face appeared in front of my car window, and my heart stopped for a second. It was Sumair; he knocked on my window asking me to open the car door. I turned off the engine and got out of the car. The street was not a busy one and not properly lit. There were a few white street lights, but they were way ahead. The lights on the banner of the club were reflecting on the road which made things visible. The girl who was by the car saw us and started moving into the darkness of the road. And the guy followed. Sumair tapped on my shoulder and asked, "What's up? Let's go?" "Yeah!" I didn't want to go; a part of me wanted to follow the couple, not as a stalker, but I was intrigued by what was going on. I wanted to know what happened. I walked towards the entrance of the club. The gate was right there; I was moving forward when Sumair just pulled me to the right. "Don't you wanna smoke before we go inside?" I didn't want to smoke at that moment, but why won't I take a step forward to ruin me; I was my biggest hater. "Yeah, let's go!" I followed him to the dark corner of the club, it was near the back entrance of the club. He stopped and turned back; he lit the joint and gave it to me. He used to be one of those guys who could never really smoke but wanted to look cool. "Where is it from?" I dragged a puff. "Manali, you remember my friend Ruchika? She got it" Ruchika? Hah. I couldn't recollect who she was, but the way Sumair bought her name up, it looked like I've met her before. I just nodded and didn't say or ask anything. I passed the joint. It's a weird feeling to have when you don't know what will happen the next minute or next day or next month. What did I have to look forward to? What was I living for? Was I high already? He threw the bud away and held my hand; his fingers were really soft. He started walking, and I was pulled by him. Nothing much changed. Things just seemed a lot more clear. The first time I ever smoked was a lot more different; for a second, I could feel every organ in my body, and the next second, my whole body was numbed. I couldn't even breathe normally. And now, it's just a little woozy feeling in my head. I sat on the couch looking at the lights. "Why is he always like this?" Ryan's girlfriend said. "Apne bf pe dhyan de bro, don't act like you're the part of this group; we don't even know your fucking name." Sumair stood up for me, like he always does; I smirked and laid my head back. Ryan sat next to me. "What's up with this? Why is Sumair again arguing with my girlfriend?" he chuckled.

"Why do you keep changing your girlfriends; it's getting difficult for us to keep up." I closed my eyes. I could hear his silence. He stood up and sat next to his girlfriend. I could hear them quarrel. Couldn't make out what they were exactly talking about. I opened my eyes to the blurry darkness. Two figures hugging each other. I came forward to grab a pint of beer. I wanted to chug it in one go, but I couldn't. I left the bottle there and walked out. It was soo peaceful, cold wind blowing through the trees, an empty road. Me walking into nothingness. I could hear my steps and my thoughts; I wasn't scared at that moment; I remember how much I used to struggle to sleep alone as a kid. These noisy trees are my peace now, but there was a time when they were my fear. Well, I could just let go of my ego and sleep next to my dad. But I didn't. I punished myself to punish him. I will punish myself every day if that makes him pay for what he did. I looked up at the moon and the stars, the trees were gushing; it got colder, and my body fell on its knees. The road was a secluded one, where hardly anyone came. I laid there looking up at the sky. Slowly the sky was falling on me. The stars started to move, and I couldn't take it any longer, so I closed my eyes. There she was standing on that balcony... I opened my eyes and stood up. I started walking towards my place. Halfway through I realized I had left my car back at the club. I smiled and kept walking and walking without realizing that I actually reached my society. I entered my society, looking at the moon and bumped into a tiny creature. She turned, and well, I would be lying if I say I didn't want to stare at her face for a little longer; it was her, the girl I saw in the evening; she was my new neighbor. I saw her face clearly for a split second, but she was there with her mother; I walked ahead, and it felt like she called me. I turned, but she was giggling with her mother. Did I look funny? I turned back and had a smile on my face. A smile I didn't force. That night I laid on my bed having hope, not the kind of hope that I will see a person tomorrow, but the kind that tells you that you are worth something more than just breathing. I entered my house, and my dad was pacing around the hall. "Where were you? Sumair called; he said you just left.." he said grabbing me by my shoulders. "I am fine" I said; I didn't want to fight him; I was feeling better today. "This behavior is not fine, Yohanne." "Okay, this behavior is not fine, and everything that you do is fine?" I yelled. "I just want you to grow up and take care of yourself." He said assertively. "Then... Fuck off" I said and walked up to my room. I locked myself in my room and threw myself on my bed. I was high and tired and a little dreamy.

The next morning... As usual, I picked myself up from the temporary death. I checked my phone, which was still dead. I plugged the charger into it. It was a sunny day; my AC was off the whole night, and the balcony was open too. The room was way too warm to continue to sleep in it. I stood up to close the balcony glass and pulled the curtains, but I got distracted by the house that never mattered to me. I was standing there still. Looking inside her house through her balcony. I knew it was a living room there, and I was pretty sure that she took the bedroom right next to the balcony. I smiled and closed the curtains. I turned the AC on and laid on the bed. I checked my phone; it had 5% battery. I left it there and went into the bathroom to get ready. I could not miss my morning cycling for anything in this world. I went down and unchained my cycle; I hopped on it and took it out of the main gate of my yard. The air on my face felt super refreshing.

I started pedaling faster. I looked at the mountain, which was extremely far yet visible from the society. I was almost there, crossing the entrance when I tripped and fell. I had fallen after a long time. It felt weird, but unfortunately, I didn't bruise myself. I got up and picked up my cycle. My mood was spoiled, and I no longer wished to cycle further. "You are going to give up?" I asked myself. I started pedaling again, faster and faster. My thoughts, my mind, was all blurred. My focus was on the wind, on my breath, and on the road. When suddenly something strange happened.

I saw that girl in my vision, in my head. I pulled the brakes and stopped at the side. I took a couple of deep breaths and looked ahead. I was yet too far from the mountain. I turned back, and I was too far from my house as well. I decided to go back that day.

I reached home and I laid on my bed and instantly fell into deep sleep. "Yohanne... Yohanne... Get up." A blurred vision of my dad trying to wake me up. "What's this, Yohanne? You've been asleep all day, get up." "What the heck do you want from me?" "Nothing, dinner is ready, just come out and eat." He turned the lights on. The temperature of my room was too low. I looked around for the remote to turn it off. I looked in the mirror on the front wall. I saw the reflection of the remote on the side table. I bent to the left and grabbed it. I turned the AC on and stretched. My body was sore, and my brain was numb.

I saw my phone; it was fully charged. I opened my Instagram. I hardly got any notifications. There was one, though, a follow request from a girl with an open account. I went through her profile, and I was very sure I didn't know her; we didn't even have any mutuals. As I was going through her profile, a picture struck my eye. I knew that girl. It was not the one who had sent me a request. This one picture belonged to my neighbor. I decided to text her. I knew that she was playing, and I was going to let her play, just by my rules. 15 minutes into the conversation and I got her friend to block me already. How cute.

I went down to eat dinner as I was starving. I was shocked at my own capabilities to sleep for that long. I reached the dining room and sat at the table. "I thought you would skip dinner again," he said. I didn't reply to his comment. I didn't like talking to him much. I grabbed a plate and served myself some boiled vegetables and paneer with rice. I was hogging onto the food. He looked at me and didn't say anything; after 15 years together, we were both used to co-living with minimal interaction. "How was the day?" He asked. I sighed and kept eating. "Yohanne? I'm talking to you," he said. "I know you are, but I'm really hungry, or I would have skipped. Can you please try and not talk to me?" I said. "Sure!" he said and started eating his food. He took a couple of bites and then went away to his room. "Awesome!" I said and took more food on my plate. I finished my dinner and left the plate there. I walked up to my room and locked the door behind me. I went out to the balcony and looked at her house; I smiled and lit a cigarette. I smoked peacefully while enjoying the chilly weather. My heart sank when a thought about my dad came into my mind. I didn't love him, but I was close to hating him. At the same time, I also felt bad for being so mean to him, but did he think twice before doing what he did to me. I threw the cigarette on the road and went back inside my room. I turned on the TV and played a random movie. I didn't realize when I fell asleep.

I got up, got ready, and went for cycling. I went on for a couple of miles, when I decided to turn back. While I was coming back, I could see her with a cycle, and it surely didn't look like she could cycle. She was struggling to even balance herself for 5 seconds, and before I could reach her, she fell. I left my cycle on the side to pick her up. I held out my hand for her to take the support and get up; she looked at me with those big eyes, and her face went pale. She got up on her own somehow and ran. She ran towards her house and locked the door. That very moment I knew it was one of two possibilities: either she was scared of me, or she had a crush on me. I took her cycle and parked it inside her yard. I took my cycle and went back in. I knew I had to figure out what it was, so I walked inside my house and sat on the couch. Took a deep breath and I started laughing, on how cute someone can be. I took my phone out of my pocket and texted on her Instagram account, which I took from her best friend's account before they blocked me. I texted her.

YO: Hope you are doing okay.

She read it that very minute, and her silence was so funny to me; I could imagine her big eyes going bigger in shock.

AL: I am okay. How did you get my ID?

YO: WELL HI, Kajal

AL: She told you??

YO: No, her profile told me.

AL: Ohhhh

YO: You still didn't get it right.

AL: Hehe

YO: Looks like you are new here.

AL: Yes

YO: Tell Al', what do you like apart from cycling?

AL: Haha stop making fun of me, I was just trying a new sport.

I had a gut feeling she saw me and tried cycling to make friends or to hit on me, but I liked the slow unfolding of the conversation.

YO: You didn't answer me?

AL: Hmm, I like painting, I like trekking

YO: Do you?

AL: Yeahh, kinda

YO: Would you like to join me for one? I mean not a proper trek, but we could walk till the top of the first mountain we find nearby.

AL: Sounds like a good plan, I'm in.

YO: So tomorrow at 7 am?

AL: Yeah, see you tomorrow.

I kept my phone aside and laid back looking at the ceiling; after ages, I didn't feel that bad about my life.

CHAPTER 6

Ahilya

It rained last night, and the day was very beautiful. It wasn't that sunny or that cold. It was just perfect; trees were dancing, and that pretty smile on Yohanne's face. Now that finally, I was getting to see him so closely. It was the best view of my life. Why was he smiling though? Well, his view was a little different; I was gasping for breath. The more I tried to breathe without making noise, the more noise my nose would make. My throat was as dry as my DMs.

Yes, my DMs were dry; I didn't have any spicy drama going on, and I was trying my best to get back in the game after Rahil and to forgive myself from breaking his heart.

Every step I was taking pulled life out of me. He was trying to keep up with my super slow walking, and I could see it on his face that he knows I'm struggling for my life. Even in this situation, I couldn't take my focus off of his calves. He stopped, and my legs thanked him. The place couldn't get any prettier.

"Let's sit here for a while?" Yohanne asked, and as much as I wanted to answer him, my body didn't support me. When I failed to speak, I decided to just nod, in agreement.

We were on a mountain, and I could see the world from above. It was beautiful and windy. When a bottle appeared next to my face. I grabbed it and chugged on it like my life depended on that water.

"You can sit on this rock, rest for a while, breathe." he chuckled. I forced myself to stop as I had to save some water for the hottie too. I passed the bottle to him, and I sat down on the big rock, making sure it didn't prick my asshole.

He sat next to me. I couldn't take my eyes off him when he started to drink water; his blue sports tee complimented his body just the way an old creep compliments a young girl on Facebook. His triceps moved under his skin. And water dripped from the side of his mouth, dropping down on his tee, which was already a little wet from his sweat. I could smell his perfume, mixed with his sweat, creating some weird intoxicating pheromone. But I smiled at him, keeping all my desires and expressions in control. He kept the bottle in his mini bag.

He looked at me, still struggling to breathe properly.

"You should always carry a water bottle."

"I'll remember that." I covered my face with my palms, trying to wipe the sweat.

"No no stop, hey." He stopped me and I took my hands down, completely confused about what I did wrong. He reached out to his bag and pulled a plastic pack of wet wipes. He pulled one out and took my right hand in his; he slowly wiped my palms one by one. Even though everything was happening at a normal speed, for me, it was all in slow motion.

"So Ahalya ha.."

"Soo Yohanne ha ..."

He smiled looking at the peaceful blue sky.

"Are you liking it here in Pune?" He looked at me, and I liked every bit of it.

"I love it here." I forgot every other possible answer to that question.

"What next?" he looked deep into my eyes; he started bouncing his legs slowly.. Biggest sign of anxiety.

"Trying to get a scholarship in this Fine arts college in Florida." he looked down like he was thinking something. His lips moved like he wanted to say something but stopped.

"Say it"

"What?" he asked, looking at me.

"You were gonna say something but you stopped, so say it"

He shook his head slowly. "Nothing... really"

There was a silence in his eyes, those beautiful brown eyes. "Go on Ahalya, I'm still interested in knowing more about you."

"Well okay, I'm a painter..."

"I figured that out... with the fine art part" I giggled, and the wind blew. My hair fell on my face. He got his fingers close to my face as if he were to put my hair behind my ears but he stopped.

"May I?"

"Yes" I had a smile bigger than ever on my face. He gently took the hair off of my face and placed it behind my ears.

"I must say you've got a gorgeous smile." He looked at my lips and back at my eyes. I blushed even more and looked down.

His hands were on his knees, and his fingers were flicking. As if he was confused if he should be holding my hand or not. I could feel a shooting pain arising in my lower back. I stretched my back, and he saw it.

"Your back is hurting?"

"Ahh no" he knew that I was lying, he smiled.

"You wanna lay down?"

"Here? On this dirty dry grass?"

"Yeah, I mean, it won't stick to your clothes for sure." Was he being serious? I kept looking into his eyes in disbelief. And he kept staring back at me.

He rolled back and laid on the grass and kept his bag under his head; he squinched his eyes as he looked directly into the sky.

I had to turn halfway to look at him. "You need an invitation?"

"I don't have a bag. Where do I put my head?"

He opened his right arm "here, if you are comfortable" I didn't know if I was but I wanted to. I laid next to him on his arm; at this point, I could smell his perfume very clearly, and it was great.

The experience was so overwhelming for me that my nose couldn't take it all, so I had to breathe from my mouth. I closed my eyes and focused on the sound of the trees and the breeze.

"Are you seeing anyone?" I asked, tilting my head a little up to be able to see his face but all I could see was his chin.

"Not really; I've never really been in an actual relationship." Why god, why? Why does every hot guy have to be a mess?

"Hmmm"

"Are you judging me, Miss Mirza?"

"Kinda, I mean why not? Why won't you get into a relationship?" I got up and turned to him.

I sat there with my legs folded, looking him straight in the eye, waiting for his answer. He got up, folded his leg, and sat in front of me, knee to knee.

"You want me to give you an answer that will not mess with your head or the truth."

"Both"

"Ahhh okayy negative or positive"

"Positive" I had this image of this guy in my mind; I didn't want him to ruin it already. I stayed put, waiting for him to speak. He took a while; maybe he was trying to come up with a way to explain himself.

"Hmm okay, now if you like a puppy, very much.."

"You're calling girls puppies?"

"No, no... no, don't take it like that okay."

"Oh well, I will take it like that okay" I wanted to scare him, but the smile on my face could not stay hidden for long.

"See it like this na, puppies are cute, girls are cute."

"Shh shush now stop defending your lame example, just finish it."

"Hmm alright, so you see when you like a puppy a lot and you want to adopt it, but you know you don't have the right environment for it to stay happy with you, so you don't adopt it, instead you play with it whenever possible and one fine day it gets adopted, and you are happy for it."

"What the literal fuck is wrong with you?" I almost yelled at him. I must say I was disgusted by this example, but at the same time, I was shocked that it actually made sense, but it's still disgusting.

"Dude, it came out really wrong; this is not what I imagined in my head... Fuck.. but wont you agree it makes sense." He started laughing; he bent down trying to control his laughter; his forehead almost touched my legs.

He grabbed my hands and got himself back up.

I was still giving him the look. Even though I wanted to laugh, what kinda feminist would I be if I laughed at such jokes.

"If this is positive, I really wonder what negative would look like."

"Sound like."

"What?"

"Nothing."

I smiled, and as I was getting up, he held me by my hands and pulled me down, not with a lot of pressure, just the right amount to make me sit again.

"Stay, don't get mad."

"You'll have to make up for it."

"How do you want me to?" He was so close to me, his fingers caressing my palm gave me butterflies in my stomach.

I didn't say anything for a good 10 seconds, and he understood that I was processing the feeling I was feeling at that moment.

We didn't look away.

"What are you doing Ahalya?" he kept looking.

"I am looking at you Yohanne."

"Are you?"

"Yes, I am."

"Do you like what you see?" and my heart stopped.

The guy I was dying to talk to was right there, right in front of me, mostly about to kiss me.

He leaned towards me; his left palm touched my cheeks gently.

We looked up into each other's eyes. He came a little closer; my hands were on his thighs. I didn't want him to kiss me. I liked him way too much to ruin it by a kiss.

Yes, kisses can ruin untouched love. I wanted to keep imagining how it would be to kiss him once I'm madly in love with him.

I could feel his hands moving from my arms to my shoulders to pull me in. Don't do it, please, don't. I closed my eyes.

Something vibrated under my palm. I opened my eyes and looked at him.

"I'm so sorry" he said, he pulled his phone from his pocket, he stood up and walked ahead. He turned back to look at me and smiled.

So basically he was going to kiss me without actually liking me. How is it so easy for guys to kiss someone?

I laid on my back, looking up in the sky, my eyes got used to the sunlight. I took a deep breath.

I was tired and sleepy. I just wanted to turn to my right and sleep there.

But I had to pull myself up and get going. The moment was gone, but it was there. Which means that something can be there.

I got up and saw him walking towards me. I took my bag and his bag and started walking towards him.

"Who was it?" No, I didn't plan on asking him that personal question, but it just moved out of my mouth, and I didn't want to think I'm one of those people who interfere a lot in others' lives.

"Yess, it was my best friend; he is singing at his own cafe tonight. I mean not just him, but he is having an event kinda thing where these indie singers will come and sing, so he will be one of them too."

"Ohh okay great, have fun."

"You won't come?"

"Am I coming?"

"Why not? I mean, it's on you, though, but I'm assuming you don't know people here, so you should come."

"Is it a date?" Why did I say that? Literally, things kept coming out of my mouth.

There was a smile on his face when he said, "Sure!"

So it was a date.

I sat on a pile of clothes, feeling completely hopeless about finding the perfect dress.

"Just wear this one!" my mom suggested, tossing a yellow and white striped dress onto the pile. I was almost in tears.

"No, mom, this makes me look like a schoolgirl," I protested. Mom threw the dress back onto the pile.

"Did he say it's a date date?" she inquired.

"I told you, he asked me if it's a date, and I said sure! So yes, it's a date, mom."

"So, on a date, he is taking you to meet his friend?"

"No, he is taking me to a music event where his friend will also sing."

"Okay, wear the dress you wore on Kajal's birthday, the black sleeveless one."

"Where is it? Why can't I find it in this pile?"

"It's an expensive dress; it's kept in my suitcase." I didn't like how my mom hid my clothes, making me forget about them.

We walked to her room, and we found the suitcase on the top shelf.

"I swear, if you don't wear it, I will kill you," my mom warned.

"Kill me, but first, can we take it out?"

"Go get the stool."

"From?" I asked, he looked at me in sheer anger. She usually wasn't mad at me for such things, but this time I messed up the house just to pick a dress.

"What will you do without me?" she asked.

"I don't know," I replied as we found the stool on the balcony.

"What is it doing here?" I asked.

"Dad got it to fix the bulb here," she explained, and we used it to reach the suitcase.

"Chadd ja," she instructed.

"Me?"

"Shut up and get on it."

I climbed onto the stool, fearing for my life, hoping not to see any lizards. Luckily, I only found the suitcase. I threw it on the bed, and we opened it to reveal my beautiful dress.

"Thank you, Mom."

"Thank me later; first, put the suitcase back."

I got ready for the date in the evening.

All set for my first date with Yohanne, I had to leave before my dad entered, as seeing me all decked up to go with a guy I barely know might make him really mad.

A text popped on my phone from Yohanne.

Yohanne: Waiting outside.

I stepped out, knowing that he will fall head over heels for me in that dress.

I saw him leaning on his car looking at his phone in that dim bluish light. I opened the gate and stepped out.

It was all so beautiful, there were no bright lights around us, a dim light falling on us from our houses. The winds were blowing and I just wanted him to take my hand and dance with me, i felt like I was walking towards him in slow motion. There was a smile on my face as I was imagining his reaction when he would see me. I was almost near him, I stood there and he was lost in his phone, my brain wasnt thinking much or may be too much that it couldn't process a single thought. His fingers tapped at high speed on his phone screen. I cleared my throat and said.

"How do I look?"

He looked up for a split second "Good" he smiled and moved to the right of the car and got in.

What just happened , I tried convincing myself that he must be in a bad mood.

I sat in his car. "You wanna play some music" he asked, i was still adjusting my dress, pulling it out, as the front flare was stuck under my butt. But i felt like i was obliged to avoid taking my time and answering him.

"What do you like?" I asked him.

"Play whatever you like, let me see." He places his hands on the steering wheel and looked at me waiting for me to answer.

"Okay let me think about what i wanna play."

I'm typically embarrassed of my music taste so I played an indie pop song. He began to drive.

I kept looking out like a child, none of us tried talking. He smelled really good but i didnt wanna compliment him as he didnt even notice a thing about me. I was disappointed but didnt wanna make it evident.

His one hand was on the wheel, one on the gear. I wanted him to hold my hand, but why would he.

Rahil would do that, why was i comparing, but he would do that, take my hand while driving. I should not think about rahil

The car kept moving and I kept getting uncomfortable. His car was very cold and my dress was literally irritating me. I kept looking outside and none of us tried talking to each other.

"All good" I decided to initiate

"Yeah its all chill dont worry"

"Hmm okay" i looked outside again.

"I don't think its all chill." I said, although I tried not talking but couldn't keep it in.

"trust me, im fine." He said but not a single cell of him looked fine.

He pulled over near a big cafe, he turned to me and looked at me, his eyes were black and shiny.

"I know weve just met but you can share"I said, wanting to touch his hands but I stopped my self.

"I wish I could Ahilya but, ive pushed it back and it wont come up." He replied .

"it is" I said.he didn't say anything for a few seconds.

"come, lets not make sumair wait."

He said and looked away. He got off his car and I followed. I looked at the café, it didnt look like a small cute cafe, it was huge and the front wall was completely glass, i could see singers through it.The music was audible till the parking lot although it was muffled

He started walking ahead and I followed, I hated it already, why would he even get me here. .

He stopped. He turned and looked at me. He pulled me ahead and placed his hand around my shoulder.

I just wanted to throw his hand off of my shoulders but I calmed myself. The place wasnt that crowded but it was lively. There were hardly any oldies there, they all looked our age.

.Yohhanne waved at someone *this could be his friend.* My eyes moved in that direction trying to see who he was waving at. I saw a 5'10 feet tall, fair complexion, cute looking guy. The guy walked towards us. His face looked very familiar, but i knew for sure i didnt know him.

"HIIII welcome bro" he hugged yohhane like two beer glasses were bumped into each other.

"This is ahalya, my new neighbor."

Right, that's all i was, his neighbor

"Hi Ahalya, im Sumair, nice to meet you, thankyou for coming today," he held my hands very gently and patted it.

"Please guys have fun, i'm next in line to sing." he took his phone out of his pocket and handed it to yohanne

"My sister will be on a video call" he walked on the stage.

Yohanne called his sister , and it seemed like they knew each other.

"Hi Yoh kesa hai?"

"Im good, he is starting to sing im turning the back camera on"

I was just there as a supporting character in the background.

Sumair got up on the stage and the lights went dim. The spot light was on Sumair and I looked at yohanne smiling, he looked so proud of his friend.

Looked around and the crowed was already cheering for him.

The music began and he started singing. His voice was smooth and heavy at the same time. I could see girls going crazy in the audience. The lyrics made sense and the song was completely new to my ears. I walked ahead to have a cleared look of him. I was lost in his music and didn't want it to end but it did. I looked at yohanne,he was already looking at me, he smiled and turned away. Sumair came down to us.

"did you guys like it?" he asked loud enough for everyone to hear it.

"we loved it" Yohanne said and handed him his phone, where his sister was there on a video call.

"thankyou dii, okay bye, will call you once im home." He said and hung up the call. He came to me with a smile.

"did you like it?" he asked.

"yes you should definetly be a playback singer." I said

"that's so sweet of You. We can be friends." He laughed , I looked at yohanne again and he didn't have a smile on his face.

"Come Yoh! Lets get a table." Sumair said pulling Yohanne. We moved to a table.

"Ahalya, will you have a coffee and nachos ?" sumair asked

"Umm sure okay"

"I'll place the order, would you mind staying here till we go for a quick smoke and come back.

"Its okay to carry on, these singers are enough for me to entertain myself."

I looked into yohannes eyes, he realized that i felt bad. He still went with him.

Sumairs phone was left on the table. And it kept ringing i didn't want to look but i still did.

It was from a girl called "Tanya"

Hmmm the sweet boy has a gf to ignore

My energies were down and the waiter placed the coffee and nachos on my table, the food felt like a compensation.

I had no will to eat. They came back and sat on the table after 15 minutes

"You look stressed ahalya, all okay ?" sumair asked

I looked at Yohanne as he stood up. "I'll just use the washroom and come back." I was alone at the table with Sumair.

"Some Tanya was calling you."

"Yeah, that 'some Tanya' is my girlfriend."

"Then call her back."

"No, umm, just forget it. Let's talk about you."

"Okay, what about me?" Finally, someone cared. "Umm, what are you like? Have you murdered someone yet, or are you planning to date someone, or are you dating someone already?"

"Hmm, how do I trust you with this information?" For some reason, I had a smile on my face. He came closer and whispered,

"Well, try me."

"Okay, yes, I am stressed. Not stressed, actually, but upset."

"Okay, why is that? What's bothering a cute girl like you?"

"I'm not that cute." I blushed and looked down. "Okay, not that cute. Tell me, what is it? I hate it when people come to my cafe with that mood." I looked up at him, biting my lips. "Well, it's Yohanne." "What?" Yohanne pulled his seat. "Nothing. I asked her who is the most handsome guy here, and she said it's Yohanne." Sumair looked at me and winked. I whispered thank you. "Yeah, I thought you are the most handsome-looking guy here, Sumair." "Yeah, but you see, my friend, that is not how it is for Ahalya." "Well, now I think I might change my answer, Sumair. I think it's you." I smirked and looked at Yohanne. "Yay, lucky me. Now finish your coffee, the two of you; I'll be back." He stood up and walked to another table. "I'm sorry; I was supposed to make you feel nice, but I've been in my own head the whole evening." "Okay, good that you noticed, and apology accepted." He placed his hands on mine and smiled. "Let me know when you wanna leave." "Soon, actually. Dad is at home, and I'll have to sneak in." "Okay, at least finish the food." "Yeah, you also eat, na." He grabbed a fork and started taking really big bites while I was just sipping on my coffee. I took a small portion on my fork; the nachos got soggy, and now it just tasted like mashed bread with salsa and cheese. My heart was at peace knowing that he is considerate.

We got out of the cafe, Sumair walked out with us. "Ahalya, would you mind if I take your Instagram?" "Sure, it's Mirzalya26." "I'll add you," he said. I had my arms around me as it was cold. "Are you cold?" Yohanned asked. "Yes, a bit. I didn't get any coat." "You could've asked na; I have one in my car. I'll just take it." He opened his car, and I looked at Sumair. He gave me a very sweet smile. Yohanne covered me from behind. "Thanks." "No problem, Kiddo." Did he just call me kiddo? We sat in his car.

I waved at Sumair while Yohanne started the car. We were on the road, and I asked him, 'Why would you call me a kiddo?'"

"Isn't it cute, though? You are like a little kid." "Hmm, okay. What do you want me to call you then?" "Ah, Daddy." Yes, that was enough to shut me up. I had an uncontrollable smile on my face; I looked ahead and then outside the window, just to avoid looking at him. "Call me Daddy, kiddo."

"Hmm, shut up, please." I closed my eyes, pretending to sleep, just so that he could look at me and think how pretty I am. "We are here, sleeping beauty." I didn't realize when I fell asleep. "Oh, I'm so sorry; I think I fell asleep." "You think? Very strong assumption." I got off the car, and he did too. I was taking the jacket off when he stopped me. "Give it to me later." He came forward and kissed my forehead. "Good night." "Good night, Yohanne." He went towards his house to open the gate. "Go, go in; I'll be fine," he said. "I had texted mom, waiting for her to open the door." "Okay." A hand tapped on my shoulder; I turned, and we smiled at each other. She knew I had a lot to tell her.

I went to my room, and as I was changing my clothes, I took off that jacket and sniffed it. It smelled like love. I hugged it and hid it under my pillow; luckily, mom didn't notice that I had it on. I changed into my T-shirt and shorts and sat on my bed waiting for mom. I wanted to text him right away, but I knew it would make me look desperate. I mean, shouldn't he be the one texting me right now? Why can't he just be the perfect guy and text me?

Mom opened my bedroom door, and she had a plate in her hand. "Yeh kya hai?" I asked

"Khaana."

"I'm not hungry; I don't feel like eating."

"It's chhole bhature! Dad got it on his way home." She raised her eyebrows, trying to get me all excited as she knows I love chhole bhature. "I'll only eat it if there's something to drink with it." Because yes, I'll only eat it if there's a soft drink at home. "Shut up and eat." "Yaar, Mumma, please leke aao na." "I hate you sometimes, Aloo." She got up and went down to get me a glass of it, and I jumped from my bed to go to the balcony and see. The lights were off; he wasn't there in his room or on his balcony. I was wondering where he went when I looked up at his terrace. He was there under the bright moonlight, looking at it, smoking something. "You were with him for the whole evening," mom said from behind; I turned and sighed. "Isn't he so dreamy?" I took the glass from her hand and took a long sip. "Well, this won't get you high." "I wanna be on that terrace." I cried. She tapped my shoulder and pushed my back slightly. We went into my room, and I just fell on my face on the bed. "Whatttt," she yelled. "I don't know, mom; I guess I'm falling." "Hmmmm, okay sure." "I wanna know your story again." "You've read the book like a million times, Aloo." "Tell me while I eat, please." "Mm, ookay, I was 22, living in Mumbai alone when I met Abhay. He was a very charming guy, but I didn't fall for him." She started with the story but I didn't know anything about Abhay, he was not even there in the book.

"What? No, this isn't there in the book. The story starts when Dad saw you at a party."

"Do you know whose party was it?"

"Oh my god, nooooo, mom, nooooo, wtf."

"Control, or else I won't tell you."

"Okay, I'm shut, I'm stuffing food in my mouth; please go on." I took a big bite and started chewing it.

"Okay, hmm, so." She pulled herself together and started the story that I had never heard. "I was 22 when I met Abhay; I used to live in Bandra, had a store, and there was a coffee shop right in front of my store. I used to love going there. So, that's where I met Abhay."

"Why didn't you marry him?" I asked

"Because you don't marry the first guy who likes you; you marry the guy you fall in love with." She explained

"That's why I'm not with Rahil." I mumbled

"Okay, then." I focused on food and the story taking my mind away from Rahil.

"Then Abhay fell in love with me, and he introduced me to his mom. She didn't like me, and she was kinda mean to me, yet Abhay would not take my side. I wasn't falling in love with him, but to be honest, I didn't know love till then. And one day, he took me to meet his best friend, and there he was. Zaid." "So it was not that party?" "No, actually. I fell in love with him a little when I saw him for the first time." "And in that party?" "Don't even ask; I had a drink, was a little tipsy when I saw him leaning on a car, and you know what my heart said, 'It's okay if I don't get you in this life. My next life is yours.'" "You did get him in this life, right?" I asked slowly, I knew what their relationship was like.

"I don't think so; I think I lost him. He is just there, alive, breathing, but it's not that person." "Do you still love him?"

"Hmmmm. Finish it and keep the plates in the kitchen." She got up from my bed, smiled at me, and left the room; she walked right into the darkness of the hall. I felt bad for forcing her to tell me that story. I didn't even feel like eating anymore. It was a mixed feeling; I felt sadness and happiness at the same time. I finished the food and kept the plate under my bed.

CHAPTER 7

Shraddha

It was a routine for me to get up and be a wife, then be a mom. I loved being a mom to my daughter, but I was a wife just for the sake of it. I made breakfast and tea for my husband; he waited for it on the table with his phone. I placed the plate in front of him. He looked at me and didn't say anything. I've had such moments in the past where I felt that he didn't love me as much as I loved him. I sat on the chair next to him, looking at him.

"How's Ahalya doing?" he asked, keeping his phone aside. "Good, I guess. She has made some friends," I said. "Hope it's not the neighbor's son." "What's wrong with the neighbor's son?" "Didn't you see he was smoking on his balcony the day we moved here? You really want our daughter to do all that?" "Well, look, we should trust our daughter a bit, okay? She is an adult now, and she knows what's good for her," I said. He looked at his watch and looked back at me; he didn't say a word. Although we lacked love, we never lacked respect; he respected my trust in our daughter. "Okay, take care," he said and got up from his chair. He walked towards the door, and I followed to say bye to him. "Do you need me to get something from the store in the evening?" he asked. "No, I'm planning to stock everything. I will leave in a bit," I said. He gently wrapped his arm around my shoulder, and

I hugged him. I held him for a couple of seconds when he left and walked away to his car. He sat inside and waved at me. His car went away, and I looked at our neighbor's house. His car was still there. I sighed and went inside. I had to get ready and find a store nearby.

I waited outside the society for my cab to arrive; I looked at my phone to check the time. Suddenly, a black SUV stopped by me. I knew that car. The glass rolled down, and I could see a familiar face wearing sunglasses.

"Are you waiting for your cab?" Yash asked. "Are you following me?" I asked and smiled. "Yes, come; I'll give you a lift to wherever you wanna go," he said, opening the door from inside for me. I looked around for a bit, looking for my cab; it was nowhere to be found. I got inside his car and locked the door.

He started driving the car, and the alarm started going off. He pulled over on the side of the road and looked at me. "What?" I asked him. He pointed at my seatbelt. I was lost in my thoughts that I didn't notice I wasn't wearing my seatbelt. I tried pulling it from the side, but all my stuff kept coming in between. "Let me help you," he said and came closer; he pulled the belt around me and locked it. I kept looking at him. He fixed it and looked up. "You're all set," he said and smiled. I looked ahead at the road.

He started driving the car, and I looked outside at the road. "So where are you taking me?" he asked. "Huh?" I was confused. "You didn't tell me where are we going," he asked again. "Oh, can you drop me to a supermarket? I need to buy groceries," I said. "Oh okay, I think there was one behind. I'll just take a U-turn," he said and took a U-turn. I looked at his hands; his sleeves were rolled up, and his hands looked very strong. I took a deep breath; my body and my mind were acting up like a young girl. But my conscience was killing me for even feeling all that.

He stopped near a store, and it felt like the 15-minute drive ended in 15 seconds. I opened the door and got off the car; I bent to look at him and waved. "Thanks," I said and started walking towards the store. It wasn't a big store, but I scanned around, and it had everything I needed. I picked a trolley and started filling it with the items on my list. I could feel my mind zoning out while looking at the tags of the things I was buying. I cross-checked in the end if I had everything; the trolley was full, and I could hardly manage to push it till the counter. I had to buy things from groceries to toiletries.

I started putting my things on the billing counter one by one; I looked at the bags, there were three big ones and one medium-sized bag full of stuff. I imagined how I will take it out to the cab. The cab I was yet to book. I took my wallet out to pay the total bill of ten thousand three hundred and sixty-five rupees. A hand came from behind and placed a chewing gum on the counter; I looked back, and it was Yash. "Ma'am is this with your bill?" the cashier asked. "Yes," I replied. I had to take my eyes off Yash. I looked at the woman making my bill; she looked like a college student, a little elder to Ahilya. I smiled at her. I pulled my trolley, and he placed his hand on the handle of the trolley. "Let me?" he said and pushed it ahead. I kept looking at him. This was something I was looking for in Zaid. At that point, I didn't see Zaid or Yash in him; all I saw was a man caring for me. I didn't have to do this alone. "Weren't you getting late?" I asked. "It's okay; it's not like you'll need to shop daily, and when you said you're going to buy groceries, I realized there will be a lot of things, and you might need help," he said, pushing the trolley out of the store. "I've parked there." He pointed at his car. I followed him. He opened his car's trunk and kept all the bags in it. He closed the trunk and showed me the way to the front seat of the car; he opened the door for me, and I sat inside. I was blushing and could feel my face getting warmer. I closed the car's door gently and walked around the car to take his driver's seat. He sat inside, and we looked at each other. He turned back to look behind before taking the car out of the parking. And I kept taking it all in. He started driving, and I was lost. He looked at me and found me lost. "So what all do you like?" he asked. "Me?" I said, getting out of my mind. "Yes, who else is here?" he said. "Hmm, well, I like old Bollywood songs, I like trying out new recipes, and, umm, I like making designs," I said, trying to remember who I was. "I love old Bollywood too, and what kind designs are we talking about here?" he asked. "Oh,

I'm an interior designer," I replied. "Nice! You must be from a very rich family?" he said. "That's very judgmental, but yeah, my dad is a builder," I replied. "What about you? What do you like?" I asked. "You," he paused, so did my heart. "You like Bollywood songs, right? Let's play some," he said, and I was confused if he really said that. He looked at me, "You asked something?" he said, as if he didn't hear my question. "Ah, I asked what do you like to do?" I asked. "I like reading very much, be it books or people," he said. "Interesting, you were gonna play music," I said; he smiled and played the radio.

As I entered the society, I looked out, and from afar, I could see Ahilya entering Yohanned car. "That's your son, right?" I asked him. "Yes, and that's your daughter?" he asked back. "Yeah, but who are those other two kids?" I asked. "Um, I don't know; Yohanne never introduces me to any of his friends." "Why?" "He is embarrassed of me." "What did you do to embarrass the poor child?" I laughed, but his smile was gone. I felt I said something I shouldn't have. "Let me help you get the bags inside," he said and pulled the car over my gate. "It's okay; I'll manage." "I'm sure; you look like a strong girl, but let me help you," he said and got off the car.

And I followed. He took all three bags and looked at me. "I wish I had one more arm, but since I don't, can you help me with that one bag?" he said. "Oh, I'm so sorry." I rushed to grab the one little bag. I took the bag and ran to open the gate. He took all the bags in and helped me put them in the kitchen. "Thanks, you were a great help," I said. "No problem," he smiled; we both paused for a moment; there was an awkward silence. "I'll get going," he said, and I nodded to that; he walked out, and I followed him. He got to his car and looked at me. I smiled and waved; he waved back and got inside the car. He left, and it didn't leave me with a void. My heart felt full after ages.

CHAPTER 8

Ahilya

I woke up with birds chirping, wind blowing through my balcony, and love in the air. Before I could even open my eyes, I was lucid dreaming about getting a text from Yohanne saying I'm the love of his life. I grabbed my phone in half sleep, smiling and happy. I could almost feel like a heroine of a romantic movie. I opened my eyes, and my phone's screen was in front of me. My one eye was still shut; I had to rub it to open it completely so that I could see the letters of my lover sent through texts.

"No letters?"

He didn't text a good morning. Who does that after kissing a girl on her forehead and promising love? It's okay, Ahalya; we can learn to give a man some space. Maybe he is high on something, or maybe he was busy getting high till late and sleeping.

I couldn't wait to do what I did next. I called Kajal.

"HIIIIIIIIIIIIII."

"OKAYYY TELL ME."

"Okay, nothing has started yet but raat ko when he was dropping me home, he kissed me on my forehead."

"Wait, shuru mein kya hua?"

"Zada kuch nahi, he was busy and not giving me enough attention."

"Red Flagggggg."

"No dude, it's okay; look, he doesn't know me yet." I got off my bed and started walking towards the balcony. The beautiful weather forced me out of bed.

"Okay, but that's what na, he doesn't know you yet, and that's why if he likes you, he should be trying to know you well."

"Ha, but if there's someone I don't know, why would I put in efforts?" I saw a cab stopping in front of his house, and a smoking hot girl came out of it.

"Kajal wait... A cab stopped in front of his car, and a very sexy, tall, gorgeous-haired girl walked in."

"See, I knew it, he is a slut."

"I need to go."

"Don't, you'll look like a stalker."

"I don't have any other option. Look, if he is a slut, then I don't wanna be his prospect, and if he is not, I don't wanna doubt for no reason."

I walked down the stairs while being on the call with Kajal. I came out of my house, took a deep breath, and started walking. His kitchen had a small window facing this side, and I was hoping if they wanna have sex, then they better do it in the kitchen so that I could know for sure that he is an asshole.

"Here's the plan, Kajal, I will walk around talking to you and pretend that I came out just for some air."

I fake laughed.

"Okay, got it."

I walked around, pretending to talk and be chill, but my heart was racing. I didn't want to see him having sex in the kitchen. I kept looking at his kitchen window with a side eye. And his front door opened; Sumair walked out, and that girl followed him.

"Kajal, I'll call you back, drama drama."

"Okay, okay, bye. Update me later." Yohanne followed them out laughing.

"Abbey tu hasna band karega." Sumair yelled in his accent; he had an accent when he spoke Hindi.

"Bro, I have no words." He continued laughing. He noticed me standing in confusion and raised his right palm. I walked to him, and he leaned a little towards my ears.

"This is the reason I don't believe in relationshit."

Relationshit? This dude is stupid. Suddenly, the two arguing in front of us disappeared, and my mind was stuck on what he had just said. Relationships aren't that bad; marriages are.

"I don't think they are shitty."

"Sure you don't; your parents got a beautiful love story, don't they?"

"Well, yes, they do, and if you wanna know more, I can give you the book my dad wrote about his love story."

"Woah, what?"

"I'm done with you," Tanya yelled, her eyes were filled with tears, making me feel what kind of guy Sumair was and what he must have done to make her feel that way.

I wanted to go and ask her, but it would be really weird to do that; I shifted my focus on her black tank top and her beautiful body. Damn, Sumair is lucky and dumb to fight with that goddess.

"Don't look at them; come, we will go out." Yohanne realized I was lost; he took my hand, and we started walking towards his car.

We sat inside the car, and I saw the two of them getting in Sumair's car. It had just rained; the roads were wet and smelled like wet mud after rains. I looked at him; he was busy plugging in his charger. He started the car and looked at me and smiled.

I felt nervous; I smiled back.

"You can say what you wanna say."

"I don't wanna say anything; I literally just got up, and you pulled me in."

"Oh, good morning, princess." It had to be the most sarcastic morning wish of my life, which was followed by a sarcastic smile.

"Oh, okay, if you wanna be mean."

"I was mean?"

"Yeahhh... Where are you taking me?"

"Just for a short ride."

There wasn't much to say.

"You slept properly last night?" Yohanne asked.

"Yeah... Why don't you like relationships?"

"Ahh, why are you stuck on that abhi tak?"

"No, I'm not stuck on that; I'm just curious to know why."

He continued driving without answering my question, and I looked at my nails to distract myself. I started biting my nails to reshape them as one looked crooked.

"Look, Ahilya, you're a pretty girl, okay, and umm how old are you again?"

"20."

"Okay, see you're 20, and you're probably looking for a deep true connection, right?"

I felt offended for some reasons I knew he was right, and yes, that's what I wanted, but I just didn't want to agree to that at that moment; I wanted to prove him wrong.

"No, that's not what I want." I looked at him, and he gave a sarcastic smile.

"Okay, so what do you want, sex?"

Chills went down my spine; I was a virgin, and well, that was not what I wanted.

"Nooo," I said, and he chuckled.

"I'm sorry, Ahilya, did I make you awkward?"

"No, I'm cool."

"Have you ever had sex?"

"No."

"Liar."

Why would he think that I was lying?

"Why would you think that I am lying?" I asked.

"Firstly, you are really cute; secondly, girls usually take time to accept that fact that they've had sex when the sex wasn't that good, and actually in some cases, they don't even accept it was good." He explained.

"Looks like you know a lot about girls, ha?"

"Yeah, I do, but I like you." He turned the car around and took a u-turn and stopped near a wine store.

"Why did we stop here?"

"Beer?" he asked, pointing at me.

"No, I'm good, and I don't think so you should be drinking in the morning."

"Okay, then even I won't; I don't wanna make you awkward."

He turned his face towards me and looked at me resting his head on the seat.

I looked at him, and I wanted to kiss him, but I didn't want our first kiss to go bad ,He leaned towards me hoping for a kiss, but even my mouth wasn't kiss-ready, and I didn't want it to happen like that. I ignored him and looked ahead at the rains.

He sat straight. "I'm sorry," he said. "No, you don't have to say sorry; it's just that." Before I could finish the sentence, I got a cramp in my lower belly.

"I think I'm gonna get my period," I said with wide eyes.

"Oh shit, what do we do now? Do you have pads?" he asked, and it reminded me that I did not. I looked at him and nodded.

"Okay, umm let's do one thing. Why don't I drop you home and get your pads, will that work?" he asked, and I nodded as a yes again.

He started the car and drove like John Abraham in Dhoom. He pulled the car in front of my house and got off the car; he walked to my side and opened the door for me.

"You go rest; I'll get your stuff." He said and got into his car again. I ran towards my house; I could hear his car leaving the area. I rushed into the bathroom and locked the door. I pulled the toilet papers and folded them into a pad and placed it on my panty like a temporary pad. I got out of the bathroom and laid on the bed. I remembered that he will come back any second. I pulled myself up to go to the bathroom again. I grabbed my toothbrush and poured paste on it. I brushed my teeth as fast as I could as I definitely can't miss this chance to kiss him. I quickly washed my face and patted it with the towel. I rushed back outside to my dressing table. I pulled out a reddish-brown lipstick and rubbed it on my fingertips. I gently applied it on my lips and cheeks. As I finished my quick makeup, I took a deep breath. I fixed my hair and went back to my bed. I laid on my bed again waiting for him. I heard his car stopping nearby. I could hear him opening the door and slamming it. I smiled and closed my eyes in excitement; I placed my hand next to my face and let the hair fall on my face.

I waited for him to come with my eyes half closed. I could hear a very muffled sound of him talking to my mom. I kept my eyes closed. I heard his footsteps coming up; he entered my room and saw me asleep. I could see him with half eyes opened. He kept the bag on the table and turned around; he was going out of my room. My plan failed.

"Hey, you got it; I'm so sorry I fell asleep," I said, stopping him.

"Hey, it's okay; you can change, and if you're sleepy, then please take rest, I'll leave," he said.

I felt stupid for pulling that. He saw my face, and he could sense my disappointment.

"I can stay for a little while, but first, you please go and change," he said, passing me the plastic pack.

I opened the bag and saw a big chocolate bar in it. I looked at him with a big smile, and he blushed too.

"Thank youuu," I said and got up for a hug. "It's nothing; I always saw it on Insta reels but doing it for the first time," he said, looking down at the floor, avoiding eye contact.

"I'll change and come." I stood up and went inside the washroom. I quickly pulled one pad out and placed it on my panty. I tried to control my cramps before going out. I took a deep breath and stood up. I washed my hands and looked at myself.

I opened the door, and he was sitting there looking at the wall.

"So tell me, princess, what do you wanna do?" he asked me, sitting back on his place, he was pretty much on the edge of the bed.

"I want to dance." I said. I didn't know why I said what I said, but he took his phone out. "Which song?" he asked. "Hmm, let me think... What about 'Cold Mess'?" I said, and he types it. As it started to play, he got up from his place and came to me.

He bowed and held his palm out for me; I slowly placed my hand onto his palm. He pulled me up and swirled me in one go; we both laughed, and he pulled me towards him. I saw his eyes that closely. His jaw, his smile, and he swirled me out again. The time got slow, and my heart beats got faster. He placed my hand on his shoulder and grabbed my waist with his one arm.

We both stopped smiling, and I closed my eyes. The song ended, and we didn't move, not even a bit. He slowly released me and walked back a few steps.

"I hope I cheered you up." He asked and leaned on the wall behind him.

"Yes, you did." I smiled at him, knowing that he did not go for the kiss when there was a clear chance.

"I'll go now?" he asked. Although I wanted him to stay, something was happening to me. Something I couldn't explain to myself.

"Yeah, yeah, please. I'll also rest for a while," I said, moving towards my bed.

CHAPTER 9

Yohanne

I got out and walked towards my house; I looked at the door, it was open, it was obvious that Sumair and Tanya were inside still discussing something lame.

I walked inside and saw them on their phones. I went up to my room to quickly use the bathroom. Before I could enter the bathroom, I took a minute to look outside the balcony. It gave a clear view of Ahilya's balcony.

I figured that she could see my bedroom from her living room. I laid on my bed but opposite to the headrest. I could see her balcony, not as clearly, but I could.

I wished if her bedroom was also designed like this.

I picked a pillow and hugged it and looked at the ceiling of my room. I took deep breath and looked at her balcony again. She was standing this time, trying to look inside my bedroom.

The second I looked at her, she looked away; I laughed and got up from my bed. My heart felt a sense of fulfillment for the first time. I walked out to my balcony, and she was still looking away.

"Heyy," I called her and waved at her. She looked at me, and we both started laughing.

I held my hand out, gesturing for her to come and hold it. She held her hand out, gesturing to reach me.

Something hit me that instant; what was I doing, why didn't it seem silly.

I took my hand back and waved her again; I turned back and entered the bathroom.

I peed and while washing my hands, I looked at my face. It looked like the face of a homeless idiot.

I decided to shave... I walked down on Tanya sleeping on Sumair's shoulders, and he was still on his phone. He looked at me and woke Tanya up, but she doesn't move much.

"Are you guys good?"

"Yeah, pretty much, she is just mad at me for not giving her enough attention."

"Sure! Why don't you give it to her?"

"I don't know; it's not like I don't want to."

"Yeah, you don't know? Really? You're with me most of the time, bro."

"Because tu bhai hai mera..." he replied, helding his hand out.

We shook hands, and I sat next to him.

"What's the scene, ha?" he asked.

"About?" I laid back on the sofa looking at him.

"Aliya, Ahilya, jo bhi hai."

"Koi scene nahi hai, bhai." I looked into his eyes to make him believe that there's nothing between me and Ahilya, but the fact was that I had not asked the same question to myself.

Was there something between me and her?

"Hmm, leave that; I'm more focused on this stupid party next month; my brother is taking over my dad's business, and my mom is expecting a lot from me?"

"What is she expecting that's a lot?" I asked.

"To learn more about business, agree to get married..." he said, raising his eyebrows.

"She wants you to marry Tanya?" I asked.

"She is fine with any girl with a good background. But that's not important; what I want from you is to come to that party."

"Main kya karunga aake, bro?"

Sumair slowly places Tanya's head on the armrest of the sofa; she wakes up, but he pats her head. "Are you good, baby? You sleep, ha." We move to the kitchen with our conversation.

"Tujhe pata hai na, it's my brother, and my mom has planned this party, and on top of that, my sister will also come. They will start comparing me and dad kitna hi support kar lenge."

"Hmmm." I pulled a cigarette out and lit it.

"I'll come, see, I don't mind, but the problem is that what will I do? Once you are busy with your family?"

"I don't know, do anything but come." His phone rang, which said "mom... I have to take this call; I don't know what the devil wants from me now?"

"Hello." He picked up the call; I kept smoking, looking up at her balcony through my kitchen window. She wasn't there.

"Haa, okay." He hung up the call and took the cigarette from my lips and started smoking.

"All good?"

"Yeah, yeah, all good; will have to run home. Isko drop karke jana hai to pick Di."

"Okay, chal, bye..." he ran out and gently got Tanya up and asked her to leave with him. I could see them but not hear anything he said to her.

The two walked through the door towards Sumair's car. I walked slowly behind them as I had to close the door. I slowly closed the door and came back inside. I didn't feel alone like I usually did. For the first time, I was feeling like I didn't need them.

I pulled my phone out of my pocket and directly opened Instagram.

I opened her text box and texted her: Hey.

I instantly got a reply from her as if she was waiting for me to text her.

Ahilya : Hey.

Yohanne : What were you doing?

Ahilya: Nothing, really, was just planning to paint something.

Yohanne : Paint me.

Ahilya : Okayyyy, will try.

Yohanne: Try? Really, I thought it would be a piece of cake for you.

Al: Well still, I'm new, and every face is different and beautiful in its own way. It's just not easy to imprint the beauty in one go.

Yo: Wow, you just made me feel beautiful; I'm blushing.

Al: Haha.

Yes, I was blushing so much that my jaw started hurting when I realized I had such a big smile on my face.

YO: By the way, will you come with me to a party?

Al: Whose party is this?

YO: Sumair's.

Al: Would he want me there?

YO: I'm sure he wouldn't mind.

Al: When is it?

YO: Next month, so kaafi time hai for you to decide.

Al: Hmmm.

YO: What hmmm?

Al: Hmm means I'm still thinking.

YO: Okay, are you done thinking?

Al: Yes, I'll come.

YO: Great, now you take some rest, call me if you need anything.

I locked my phone and laid back completely on my sofa; I closed my eyes holding a cushion near my chest.

I could see her smile, her hair, and I could feel her presence around.

A scene flashed in front of my eyes of my dad hitting a mirror and breaking it into pieces; his bleeding hand crying out the name "Divyaa."

I opened my eyes in a heartbeat and looked up. My heart was racing, and every part of my body felt the discomfort.

I closed my eyes again, trying to distract myself from that vision of my dad.

CHAPTER 10

Shraddha

"Bye maa, see you in the evening."

"Byeee, have fun."

Ahilya sat in his car and made herself comfortable. Yohanne looked at me and waved. I hoped that I made the right decision letting her go with this guy. I shut the car's door for her. It reminded me of my time. Yohanne started the car, and slowly it disappeared. I started walking towards the main entrance of the society, which was quite far from where I was standing. The winds were cold, and the sun was setting. I could just feel alive at that moment. It reminded me of the time when I was 23 years old, new in Mumbai, struggling to get a life, and now here I am. With a daughter and a husband who once loved me to death, and just as the sun will fade soon, his love also did.

I had barely walked for a minute when a car went past me and stopped. I didn't turn behind as I knew whose car it was. I kept walking; I could hear the car door being opened and then shut behind me.

"Shraddha!" a familiar voice called my name from behind.

I turned to look at it, pretending that I didn't know it was him. My heart skipped a beat as it was in the mix of feelings. Yash smiled at me while walking towards me. "Hey, going for a walk?"

"Not really walk walk, just trying to breathe better." He smiled; the setting sun was lighting half of his face. And our hair was flying with the cold wind. "I'll park my car and join you?" he asked.

"Okay, I'll wait." He sprinted to his car and drove it as fast as he could. I had forgotten how it felt to wait for somebody. As I had waited for someone who never intended on coming back. I could still see that he parked his car where Yohannes' car was parked. He got off the car and walked towards me and stopped just a couple of feet away from me.

"Hi," he sighed.

"You look tired," I said, looking at his eyes.

"Yes, I am a bit."

"Toh please go get freshen up."

"No, it's alright; I would love to join you, you vese bhi look alone."

"I just thought I was alone; I didn't know I looked alone too."

"Ohhhh, sorry, didn't mean to be that deep." I hit him slowly on his shoulder for trying to tease me like that; I saw his eyes, and they were fixed on my eyes.

"Can I have this walk with you?"

"Sure." We started walking slowly towards the park...

"You're really gracious."

"Yeah, that's the compliment you give a 45-year-old woman."

"I'm a 48-year-old man, so yeah, that's all I got."

"You are a very nice man yourself, Yash."

"Ahh, how formal; can we chuck this formality?" he asked and looked at me.

"Okay, now what?" I asked, still smiling, looking at him.

"Now we become friends; you give me gossip, I give you gossip," he said while trying to wink at me.

"Hahaha, you all men just generalize women; we all don't just gossip."

"Yess maam you don't, but I do... I need a friend to gossip," he cleared, and I started laughing and snorted. He started laughing at that. I covered my face gently while laughing with my right palm. As I took my hand down, he held it. "I gotta tell you there is a light in your eyes when you smile."

"Alright." I took my hands off and started walking ahead.

"Why did your wife leave you?" I asked without realizing the question could trigger him; the smile vanished from my face, and I looked into his eyes with a serious look.

"Because..." he said and paused.

"Because?" I asked.

"Because, Shraddha, I gossiped too much." I started laughing again, and he laughed too. "Okay, well on a serious note... she was too attached to Canada, and I was too attached to Pune. I tried living there with her, but it just didn't work out." We started walking slowly around the park.

"Okay, does she visit?"

"Not really."

"Why not?"

"Umm, I'm so sorry; it's just something I feel is way too personal to her for me to disclose."

"Oh, I'm sorry for being so nosy."

"Arrey, it's alright." We walked a couple of feet without saying anything.

"May I ask about you and Zaid?"

"Yes, well, me and Zaid were crazy for each other."

"Were?"

"Yes, we were. It's just gone; we grew apart."

"Do you miss it?" he questioned.

"What is there to miss?"

"The feeling of being able to feel something." I looked at him; the sun was almost down, and the sky was half red, half purple. I wanted to tell him that yes, yes I do miss feeling alive, and I do miss the feeling of being able to feel.

"I do feel" I said and he didn't say a thing

"I am alive, Yash, I'm very much alive."

"Yes, so am I," he said, and I looked away, continuing the walk. "So can two alive people be friends?"

"Hmm, I guess so." I smiled at him. "Soo do you miss her?" I asked

"I used to, but slowly it faded." He paused

"I have a confession" he continued

"Like I don't wanna cross any boundaries, but..." he stopped. And my heart stopped too. I was so confused if I wanted him to go on or stay quiet, as I knew what was going on. I looked into his eyes, and I asked myself if I really like him or I just miss the feeling of being connected?

"But?" I asked, but I didn't want him to answer.

"But nothing, I really liked this. How peaceful it is to just enjoy an evening, right."

"Yes, it is." Only if I could hold his hand and lean on his shoulder, this evening would be perfect.

I looked at him and stopped; he stood still in front of me in confusion. "I'm so sorry, Shraddha; I'm just being really silly?" he said.

"About what?" I asked; he looked at me and took a pause.

"You want me to say?" he asked.

"What?" I asked.

"Something is happening to me lately." He said, something was happening to me too, but I didn't want him to say it because if he said it out loud, I would know what he feels, and I will have to lie to him. I was too scared of his truth.

"No, don't say." I interrupted him. He looked down and then looked back up at me.

"Yes, it'll be better this way." He smiled. "Shall we continue the walk?" He asked and showed me the way ahead. I started walking, and my heart was sinking. I was feeling something deep, and I was fighting with myself that this can't be love. I can't fall in love with a person by just meeting him a few times.

"You know, Shraddha, you have a beautiful smile," he said, and I turned back to look at him with a sad face.

"What happened?" he asked.

"I tried, Yash; I'm so tired," I said, and a tear fell on my cheek; he slowly wiped it with his thumb.

"You can tell me," he said and came a little closer.

"I don't know what I'm going to do right now, but I'm just so confused, and don't judge me," I said and gently placed my head on his chest, placing my hands on his back. He took a deep breath and hugged me back. My heart stopped, and my brain screamed. What are you doing? I left him that instant. "I'm so sorry," I said, almost in tears; I didn't know what the man standing in front of me would think of me, but we both stood still looking at each other. Hoping to turn back the time and change things. But they were never in our hand. He took my hand in his hands and the sun dawned.

CHAPTER 11

Ahiilya

"That woman you see is Sumair's mom; she is kinda evil," Yohanne pointed at a woman who was wearing a white poncho. "Okay... these people look super rich," I looked around, stunned by the beauty of the place. They had chandeliers and clear white walls with wooden interiors. Everything looked super expensive. "That is Sumair's Dad with the brother who is taking over the business," I looked at the two men in tuxedos. I straightened my back and fixed my posture to mix up with the crowd. I wore black loose-fit pants with a black satin shirt, and the whole outfit would've cost me around 10k, yet it looked cheaper amongst the people I was with.

A server came to me with a tray that had three glasses of champagne. "Wow," I mumbled. "You drink!" Yohanne exclaimed. "Yeah, kinda," I avoided eye contact. "Why didn't you drink like this with me?" he asked. "Because..." before I could finish, he interrupted. "I had just woken up, and it was early in the morning. I've heard this story; anything else you got?" I didn't, so I said nothing. "Tanya nahi aayi?" I asked Yohanne. "Nope, she got some audition," I was trying to focus on what Yohanne was talking about when I saw Sumair's mother walking towards us. "Hey Yoh, look why is she walking towards us?" I asked, as I didn't know how they greeted rich people. I could follow the movies and give her two kisses in the air, but I didn't want to. "Yohanne! How are you!" She opened her arms to hug him, but only hugged him halfway, and yes, he kissed her in the air. She had a weird slow accent, like she would speak very slowly, dragging each word to its death. "Hi Sulagna Aunty." "Oh, this must be your girlfriend, right?" She did the same to me, opening one arm as if she would hide me in her poncho but leaving the hug and the kiss in the air for the ghosts in this beautiful mansion. "Hello Auntie." "Have fun, kids, and let me know if Tanya comes in; I've been waiting to see her since last month. Is everything okay between her and Sumair?" she asked. "Yes, you don't need to worry; they stopped by yesterday, and I've fixed it." He held her hand and patted it, reassuring her. "Thank you, son." She smiled at us and left, and I looked at him with my cheeks all red. He turned towards me. "And why are you blushing?" he asked, but how could he not know the reason. "Just like that," I said. So was I his girlfriend? I asked myself this question, knowing that he hadn't asked me to be his girlfriend yet. "I don't know why I thought or to say assumed that Sumair's mother didn't like Tanya." "I know why," he said. "Why?" "Because I called her evil." He reminded me. "Yes, you planted this in my head. But why did you?" "Because she is evil towards our boy." "Woah, so she is sweet to Tanya and rude to Sumair?" "Yes." "Whyyy?" "Because his elder brother Samar is taking over the business, and Mrinalini, their eldest daughter, got married to a super rich guy. But Sumair..." "Got into music and opened a café!" "Yes, and if I were Sulagna, I would be disappointed too." "Yes, cause you are a bitch." Sumair came from behind and hugged him. "So disappointing Sumair." Yohanne hugged him back. "Hey Ahilya, so glad you could make it!" he gave me a shoulder hug and continued talking. "Was he boring you with my family drama?" Sumair asked. "Are you okay with people knowing your family drama?" I asked him back. "Absolutely I am; they can reach my family; they can't reach me." "It doesn't make sense; you're saying this just to look cool." I gave him a smirk. "And I don't like you," he said and pulled Yohanne aside. I felt like I took it too far; I shouldn't have said that. I started to walk away from them as they wanted some privacy. I was looking around the house when I laid my eyes on Mrinalini. Sumair's sister, she was thin and tall and was wearing a white gown; it looked like it was designed specifically for her. She looked at me, and for no apparent reason, I was petrified. She smiled at me, and my blood melted. I smiled back at her, trying to be as elegant as she was. "What are you doing?" Sumair said from behind. "Just looking around, trying not to get bored." "Hmm, I hate it that you are bored; come let me show you my room." He pulled my arm. I resisted a bit and asked, "Where's Yohanne?" "He is already up, come," he pulled me towards the stairs and stopped near a server for a quick second. "Get a bottle of champagne in my room with three glasses," and started walking again. He had loosened the grip on my arm, expecting me to now walk on my own. I turned back to look if anyone noticed and I saw Sumair's mother looking at me, and then she looked at Mrinalini and passed a look with a smile. I turned towards Sumair and kept walking. We reached his room, which was extremely big and royal. The curtains were covered the full 10ft walls, and the floor had Carrara white marble. Apart from a huge bed, there was a big sofa and a center table. On the left, there was a huge wardrobe, and next to it was a glassy wooden door, which looked like an entrance for a bathroom. "How can one chill in here?" I asked. Sumair walked next to the bed and just fell on it. "Like this," Sumair said in a muffled voice. "Come just throw yourself on the bed." He turned his face towards me and said. "No, but wait, where is Yohanne?" I asked looking around and walking around his room. "Bathroom mein hoga ya bahar hoga, you come here na." He sat on the bed and asked me again. I walked towards the bed and sat on the edge of it. "You know you can sit comfortably, right? I'm not a classist like my parents; I don't judge my poor friends," he said in a witty manner and I burst into laughter. My hands were placed on his bed when he slowly touched my finger, and we heard a knock on the door from behind. It was the server with a bottle of champagne and three glasses. I felt very uncomfortable; although last time was different, I was confused if he was catching feelings for me. The bathroom door opened, and Yohanne came out of it.

I smiled at him, remembering how he said I was his girlfriend. He came and sat next to me while Sumair was opening the champagne.

"Are you okay?" Yohanne asked, putting his hand on mine, and I felt great.

"Yes, I'm okay!" I assured him with a smile; I could feel that my eyes were shining at that point, and he could see it.

"You look happy? Is it the alcohol?" he laid back, pulling me next to him.

"Normally I would have said get a room, but since you nasty people are already in my room, I will say get a different room, guys." Sumair just pushed Yohanne's legs aside, making room for himself. He passed glasses to us, and although I didn't want it, I just took it.

There was a moment of silence, and we just looked at each other, expecting someone to speak. I took the responsibility of destroying the silence.

"When did you guys meet?" I asked, looking at the two.

"Guitar classes!" Sumair said with bright eyes staring at Yohanne. It brought a smile to Yohanne's face too; he kept his eyes still on his feet.

"It was my first day when I saw this guy, Yohanne was such a wannabe emo kid," Sumair continued.

"What do you mean by that?" I asked looking at Sumair and then looking at Yohanne, expecting a reaction from him. He looked up at me and smiled but said nothing.

"I'll tell you Ahilya, he had long hair which he would tie into a bun, and he would only wear black clothes, and I'm sure he wanted to learn guitar to match his persona. I guess we were 17 at that time."

"Okay, you're telling me about when you saw him, not about how you became friends," I asked.

"Oh yes, so basically, this wannabe rockstar sucked at playing guitar, and I offered to help. I introduced him to my friends, and since then, we are bros," he said, holding his fist up to give him a fist bump, but he didn't give it back.

"Hmmm," I looked at Yohanne, and he had his eyes closed, the room was very chilly. I chugged the remaining drink and kept the glass on the side table. Yohanne had fallen into a deep sleep till then, and it was just me and Sumair again. I remembered the awkward little scene that took place.

We looked at each other, and Sumair came forward and laid next to me, holding his phone up on his face.

"Can I get your Instagram ID, Ahilya?" he asked.

"I gave it to you the last time we met" I said

"Sorry I didn't add you back then, didn't seem like you were important." He said

"That's so mean sumair" I said and he laughed.

"You can check; I'm added on Yohanne's," I replied, moving slowly, trying to get off of the bed.

"Okay, found ya! Next week is Yohanne's birthday, no sorry not next week, it's on the 16th," he calculated the dates on his fingertips.

"Yeah pretty much next week," I replied.

"We will do it in my café, at 12 am so be there! Since you are his new close friend nowadays so," he said and it intrigued me to ask him about the incident that happened during our interaction with his mom.

"Can I ask you something since you know Yohanne well?" I asked.

"Yes, sure, ask na."

"So earlier your mom came and started talking to us, and she said, 'Oh hi Yohanne, this must be your girlfriend,' pointed at me and he didn't say no." I said all that in one breath.

"Aww, sweety, I so don't wanna be the one to burst your bubble," he said.

"You sound so gay saying that, Sumair soo gay" The minute I said that in anger, it hit me that I was being sexist.

"I'm so sorry I didn't mean it."

"Hahaha, chill but just so you know Yohanne didn't say anything because he just didn't want another question from my mother."

"Okay, bubble bursted! Happy?"

"No look, I'm not your enemy; I'm your friend come here." He came closer and kept his hand around my shoulder.

"Look, Yohanne's birthday is coming, right? Give him a gift that matters, and maybe you'll get closer to him," he said.

"Okay, what do I get him?" I asked.

"Hmm okay I was planning to give this but you can; he was extremely close to his mom and there's a picture of him and his mother on his 3rd or 4th birthday, his dad must be having it. You could get it framed and give him." He suggested.

"So I'll have to get the picture from his dad?" I asked.

"Yes, you'll have to, and also you'll have to come help me set the party up." He said.

"Okay, I'll come." We turned and looked at Yohanne; he slowly opened his eyes.

"Good morning sleepy beauty!" Sumair said and hit him almost on his dick.

Boys are so different with their guy friends I felt, I giggled, and Yohanne looked at me.

It was around 9 pm when Yohanne and I entered the society, in his car. The lanes were dimly lit with the street lights, and the car was really cold. I was waiting for Yohanne to make a move but obviously, I knew that I will have to wait till the end of the ride. But also I was panicking hinking that what if my dad sees us kissing.

"All okay?" he asked, looking at me and then back at the road.

"Yeah, all good. I have a weird habit of thinking myself into a panic attack," I replied.

"Hmm, what is it?" he asked. I wanted to tell him that I was thinking if he would kiss me, but also that there's a chance my dad would catch us and then he would be disappointed in me.

"Say?" he asked again. Before I could say anything, he stopped the car. We had reached our destination. I decided to wait and see if he wanted the same thing. I looked into his eyes, and he slowly leaned towards me. I knew that this kiss was going to be great, but just to save myself from a situation at home, I decided to take a quick look through the rearview mirror.

"WHAT THE FUCK!" I yelled, loud enough to push him away just with my voice.

"What?" His eyes got all serious, and he looked in the mirror too.

"Is that your mom? Walking with my dad ? holding hands "

"Yes, are they friends?" I questioned

"Why are they holding hands?" Yohanne kept shooting questions at me like I'm a tarot card reader.

"Will you please shut up?they are non holding hands their fingers are merely touching and I have a dad, okay, and don't you know ek ladka aur ladki dost bhi ho sakte hai!" I said, yelling back at him.

PERFECT STRANGERS | 113

"Yeah sure, that's why you said 'WTF' so loudly. You clearly believe what you are saying."

"They are coming this way. Should I just get down? Will she get awkward?" I asked.

"The best way to figure if they are just friends or something is up: you get down casually and see if she gets awkward," he replied.

"I'm not sure if I want to do that to my mom." I actually didn't feel like busting her like that, after all, she has always been supportive of all my decisions.

"Cool, but I will."

He got out of the car, and I followed. He looked dead into his father's eyes and slammed the door. He looked at me and said, "Bye! I'll see you tomorrow." I was still a bit astonished and looked at my mom. She was giving an awkward smile to Yohanne when he said, "Bye, aunty." And he walked inside. I moved towards my mom and smiled at her. I was waiting to see if she would turn to see Yohanne's dad, or she would walk inside with me straight. She didn't turn back, but I did, and he was standing right there looking at us. I waved at him slowly, and he waved back. Yohanne was long gone inside. If Yohanne's dad liked my mom, he surely liked her more than Yohanne liked me.

CHAPTER- 12

Yohanne

I walked across the yard to my main door and realized that I didn't even look back, not even once to say bye to Ahilya. I turned back, but she was gone, and the only person standing out there was someone I hated the most.

That's when it struck me that he was with Ahilya's mother. I opened the door and walked inside. I knew what I was going to do. I was going to make a scene. I left the main door open for him to walk in.

I stood still between the living room and the entrance when I heard the door opening, followed by his footsteps.

"What were you doing with her mom?" I asked him.

"Excuse me?" He said, looking at me in confusion, but I wasn't confused. I could never leave a single chance to show him how much I resented him.

"What were you doing with Ahilya's mother?"

"I don't think I need permission from my son for talking to my neighbor, right?" he casually walked past me. It felt like he did not care about me or my feelings. I looked at the table next to me and kicked it as hard as I could. It made a loud thud noise, and he stopped.

"When will you grow up, Yohanne? When will you stop being so insecure? If there's something making you feel uneasy, talk to me," he said as if everything was okay and as if everything he was going to say was fine.

"It's not okay that I have to be alive to be this miserable. You make me feel miserable every day, every minute, and I just wish you die," I could feel my anger coming up looking at his face. He didn't say a word.

"How are you so okay after what all you have done?" I asked him as his silence was killing me. He walked back towards me, and I started moving backward too as I was disgusted even by his presence.

"What do you think I've done that's so bad?" he asked, his eyes begging for sympathy.

"Huh, sure you don't know. I don't want to look at you right now," I walked past him towards the stairs.

I climbed up as fast as I could. I was palpating, my heart could just come out of my mouth. I kicked the door open of my room and entered in fury. It was dark, with some street lights coming from the balcony. I slammed it behind me when I saw a glass on my table. I grabbed it and slammed it towards the floor but it shattered in my hand and a few pieces slit into my palm.

"Aaahhh, relax Yohanne, relax, it'll be all right. Ahhh," my eyes could no longer keep the tears in.

I hated him even more at that point for not coming in; I was sure that he had heard the noise of the glass breaking.

I sat on my bed, taking out the pieces one by one. My eyes were blurred due to the tears filling them up. I no longer needed to go back to my mom. I realized I no longer needed him either. It was just me in this dark place in my head which would not release me.

I managed to take out all the pieces and threw them on the floor. I laid back on my bed with my arms open.

"Ahilyaaaa," I didn't know why I took her name, but it gave a sense of relief to my heart.

"Where were youuu?" I closed my eyes, but the pain won't let me rest. Her face popped up in my vision, but the thought of her liking Sumair struck me; I could visualize them being happy together.

I opened my eyes and got off my bed. I walked out of my room. I was looking for my dad's whiskey. As far as I remember, he kept it in the kitchen, in one of the top shelves.

I started opening all the shelves, one after the other. My blood dropping everywhere around the floor and on all the cabinets. "We were going to kiss today, only if he didn't ruin it," I mumbled in anger.

I found the bottle in the second last cabinet. I opened it and poured it on my wound.

"Ahh," it burnt my soul, and the pain got unbearable. I straight went to the sink and washed it with water.

It slowly mellowed down. I grabbed the bottle with my left hand and chugged the whiskey. It slowly burnt my throat and my intestines till I could no longer keep it in. I threw up and lost consciousness.

I opened my eyes the next morning on my bed. My head was killing me, and my mouth wasn't making any saliva. I slowly looked around and saw a bottle of water on my side table.

I got up slowly with immense pain in my whole body, especially eyes and head. My palm was burning when I tried to use it to grab the water, but somehow I took it. I started drinking it and slowly could feel my organs coming back to life.

"You were throwing up all night," I heard my dad's voice from behind. Thanks to you is what I wanted to say, but my mouth won't support my brain. I just gave him a look and started drinking more water.

"I'll get another bottle; you are badly dehydrated." He just stood and left me alone in the room.

I rested back, thinking about the night before, how I was thinking about Ahilya.

"Are you missing me too?" I asked her, imagining her sitting in front of me. "I'll give you everything," a smile came on my dried lips thinking about her. That's when it hit me. If my mom can leave me, then anyone can. Why would she be with a person like me? I had noticed Sumair's interest in her. I knew that he was anyway going to break up with Tanya soon, and I felt that he might want to be with Ahilya.

"Will you leave me too?"

How weird that she made me smile a moment back, and the thought of her not choosing me sank my heart.

I kept looking at the wall, lost in my thoughts when dad entered.

"Here, take these. You need to finish this bottle with electrolytes in an hour, then slowly finish this other bottle; it has normal water. I'm going to the clinic and will see you in the afternoon. Please don't hurt yourself.

Can you just fuck off again? My mouth didn't support me, and I had to settle with just giving him a look.

The house was so quiet that I could hear him walking to his room, then taking his bag from the table. He opened the main door and locked it behind him. I was again all alone. I looked at the time, and it was 1 pm.

I took my phone, and there were no messages from Ahilya. I clicked on her profile, and Sumair was listed as our mutuals.

"Of course."

I closed my eyes to take a deep breath before doing that. I typed "DIVYA SINGH.C"; all the options laid in front of my eyes. My option was the first one.

I clicked on it, and the page opened. The most recent post read, "Me teaching my son about Indian pooja," the video played, with her sitting and teaching her 12 years old white son Hindi.

"Jai say om bhoor."

"Um, bhoor," I swiped up as I couldn't take any of that bullshit. I saw her pictures with her kid.

"You didn't fight for me, Mom. You didn't. She is gone, just like you did," I banged my head slowly on the wooden headrest of my bed. My deep agony was disturbed by the doorbell, but I was in no position to go down and open the door. I kept my eyes shut, feeling tears rolling down my cheeks and falling on my chest.

The doorbell rang again. I opened my eyes, wanting to kill the person disturbing me. I managed to get up from my bed. I looked at her balcony, but she wasn't there. I sighed and started walking. Each step was painful. My T-shirt had stains on it. I decided to change it before going down, but before I could do that, the doorbell rang again. My blood was boiling at this point. I took the T-shirt off and walked down to the main door as fast as I could. I looked around while crossing the living room; it all looked clean.

I reached the door, and the doorbell rang again. "Coming," I said in utmost anger. I unlocked the door and opened it. It was her, standing in a white cotton dress, with open hair tucked behind her ears. That's when I realized I had fallen in love with her. I looked at her. My senses stopped, time slowed down, and we were just looking at each other. I smiled, and then she smiled. I wanted to hug her, but I realized I was stinking.

"Hi!" she said slowly, innocently. "Hi..."

"How are you? I was worried you didn't text me last night," she said, looking at me with those puppy eyes. I could see that she was upset with me for not trying to connect with her.

"I'm so sorry, Ahilya. I was just stuck with things," I replied, holding the door open for her. She looked at the bandage on my palm.

"How did that happen?" she grabbed my hand and looked at it; her eyes changed, she looked at me with tensed eyes. I kept looking at her, taking in all her expressions. It had never happened to me before. I could smell her perfume; I just wanted to fill my lungs with her perfume.

"Did something happen last night with your dad?" she asked again.

"Hmm," I didn't have much to say. I wasn't so proud of what I did last night.

"What hmm? What did you do?" she asked again, curious more than ever.

"I guess I just lost control," I replied, looking down. It was difficult to make eye contact while admitting something like this.

"What do you mean that you lost control? Are you okay? Did he do this to you?" she flooded me with questions.

"You wanna come in?" I asked her, and she nodded. She walked inside, and I locked the door behind her. I was looking at her from behind, admiring her brown wavy hair. She turned back.

"Are we sitting here or in your room?" she asked.

"My room is a mess; can we sit here?" I directed her towards my living room. It was barely lit, with the lights coming through the white curtains. I opened the curtains and turned the lights on. I wanted to make it as bright as possible to be able to see her face. I looked at her sitting on the couch; I just wanted to kneel on the floor on both my knees and hold her hands and tell her everything.

"Do you need something?" I asked her; she looked up at me and smiled with a little nod.

I realized I was shirtless, and it could make her feel awkward.

"I'll just go quickly and put something on?" I asked her; she looked at my chest and blushed slightly and looked down awkwardly. "Yes." I ran up as fast as I could; I opened my cupboard and pulled the first thing I could find, a black cotton T-shirt. I put it on and sprinted back to the living room. I saw her looking at her phone, and there was a smile on her face. "It must be her friend; don't worry... relax, Yohanne," I said to myself. I walked up to her and sat next to her.

"Hi!" I said with a smile. "Hmm, now will you answer me?" she looked pissed.

"I will!" I replied with a smile; I was just happy I was sitting next to her.

"Are you upset with your dad because of last night? Because I think you shouldn't be mad at him. My mom told me that she came out for a walk and she found him walking outside too. I mean, this is such a stupid thing; I even felt stupid asking her that, and you here got mad at your dad and this... this, I don't even know what you did exactly, but I'm just guessing." She kept talking and talking, and I could not take my eyes off her eyes, her nose, her lips.

"No, I wasn't mad at him, Ahilya; it was dark in my room, and the glass fell off my side table." I lied, expecting her to believe it and calm down.

"Don't you dare gaslight me; you just told me outside that you lost control." She said with an angry tone.

"Okay, I'm sorry I did that to myself. I'm not mad at my dad for that." I replied softly; I wanted to just treat her as softly as possible. She was the only precious little thing I had.

"Okay, now another thing I wanted to ask you, and you might judge me for that, but I just wanted to clear it out." She said, looking at me and then breaking the eye contact.

"Go on," I said, and it made me a little nervous.

"Yesterday..." she paused, and I was hoping she would not say anything like yesterday I kissed Sumair or I fell in love with him.

"Yesterday?" I asked.

"Yesterday when Sumair's mom called me your gf, why didn't you clear it?" She asked me, and I could not guess what she was hoping to hear. It was the moment for me to tell her how I felt. She kept looking at my eyes with no expression on her face. I took her hand in my hands.

"Ahilya..." I took a deep breath. "Okay, I'll tell you." I continued. Before I could start telling her, her phone vibrated. "One second, I'm getting a call," she said; her face changed, she had a smile on her face, she stood up

PERFECT STRANGERS | 123

and went to the corner to talk to the person on the other side of the call.

I kept looking at her and waiting for her to come back. She turned back and gave me a mischievous smile. I smiled back at her.

"Okay, bye, Sumair," she said and hung up the call. She came back to her place, and she looked happy, like something he said changed her mind.

"I just said that to avoid counter questions." I replied; although it was a lie, I just could not tell her the truth. I could not burden her with my love. I could not take that smile from her; she would never be happy with me.

"Oh, okay, cool," she sighed and smiled at me again.

"I'll go now?" she asked. Every inch of my body wanted her to stay.

"You gotta go somewhere? I can drop you?" I asked her.

"I wish I could ask you to drop me, but I will figure out." She said, making a sad face.

"Where are you going?" I asked; I was intrigued to know now.

"Ummm," she took a second to think if she can tell me or not. "I'm going to meet Sumair," she said, and it pierced my heart. I had to control my tears.

"Oh, okay, you guys have become good friends, huh?"

"Yes, kinda. You can actually come to drop me till the society gate; it's really far, and I could use some company." She was still smiling. How could I be jealous of her being happy; she deserved it.

"Yes, ma'am, I'll come with you." I got up from the sofa and gave her my right hand; she looked at me and then at my wound. "Ah, sorry," I changed my hand and gave her my left hand. She held it with her soft fingers, with light pink nail polish and a thin silver ring. I pulled her up, and she stood really close to me. I didn't move back, and she stayed like that as well. I could feel her breath getting heavier; she looked down, trying to avoid eye contact. I kept looking at her. I slowly grabbed her by her waist. She kept her other hand on my shoulder. She looked at me, and I leaned in. She moved a little back and then rested her head on my chest. I wrapped her with both of my arms, and she held me back. We stood there still. Feeling each other's heartbeats.

"I gotta go, Yohanne," she mumbled.

"Why?"

"I don't know."

"Then don't, stay like this," I tightened the grip. You gotta let her go, a voice said to me. And I left her.

She looked at me confused. "Come, I'll drop you till the main gate." I grabbed her hand and pulled her.

CHAPTER 13

Ahilya

"You were right; he was just avoiding counter questions," I said, sipping coffee. Sumair and I were sitting at the table, exactly in front of the empty stage in his café. He was lost in his phone, and I was lost in my thoughts, thinking about that hug but also focusing on his words.

"I hope he heals from the wound his dad gave him," Sumair said, looking at his phone and typing something. He turned the phone screen towards me. "How's this? For Yohanne's birthday?" He showed me a picture of a PS5.

"I don't know. What wound?" I asked.

"So basically, he was 6 when his dad took sole custody of him to take revenge from his mother and brought him here," Sumair explained with pity in his eyes. "So he can't call her or meet her now? I mean, how unsettling."

"Okay, his mom was not allowed to text him or call him until he was 18; I don't know the details. But when he tried reaching out as a kid, she never picked up. Later he found that she got married to a white man, and he would just blame his dad," he sighed after finishing the whole story in one breath.

"Okay."

"Now, if you are done, can we start planning AL?" he said in a frustrated tone.

"No, I'm not done, Sumair. Okay, listen," I said, poking him with my finger. He turned towards me and sighed; he just didn't want to talk to me or discuss the situation. He had just made up his mind that this is nothing but my illusion.

"Hmm, I'm listening," he said, gently placing his hands on mine.

"So, I went to meet him today before coming here, and there was this moment between us," I said, hoping that he would understand that it wasn't just in my head; there could be something in his heart too.

"Aww, look at your eyes all tensed up; relax, sweetie. Okay, tell me what moment was it? What did he do?" he pulled me in for a hug. I felt a weird connection with him.

"I think he likes me but not that much," I said, still hugging him.

"Okay, I understand, but you like him, right? You like him a lot," he said, looking at my face while still wrapping me in his arms.

"Hmm," I had nothing to say, just a sense of losing something I wasn't sure I had.

"Isn't it so difficult being confused about all these feelings?" he said, showing a completely different side of himself to me.

"Yes, it is," I nodded, agreeing to what he said. "We still have time, right? We have a lot of time, Ahilya, he is not going anywhere, and you have all his attention, to be honest. So there's hope," he said, patting my hand.

I kept looking at him, expecting him to speak more. For the first time, I was enjoying his company and his words.

"Can we start with the plan now?" he said, and I dropped my body on the table.

"Come on, Ahilya, don't be a procrastinator. I didn't call you for this," he said, pulling me by my arm, and he stood me in front of the stage.

"Okay, what are we supposed to do?" I asked.

"I was planning a portrait of him here," he pointed towards the side of the stage.

"I can paint that," I exclaimed. He looked at me shocked. "You paint?" he asked.

"Yeah, I do," I replied. "Of course, you have to paint it, but make it big, okay? And also don't forget you have 4 days to go."

"Yeah, I know," I sighed. "So what's the plan exactly? We call him at 12 am, then what?" I asked.

"Then nothing; we cut the cake and we go home," he smiled.

"That's boring, but okay... is Tanya coming?" I asked and saw the expression change on his face.

"No, she isn't," he said. "Why..." I asked.

"We are not together, Aaliya " I noticed that he took the wrong name like usual, but I didn't want to correct him. This change in his words had a reason.

"Did you love her?" I said and turned towards him. He looked at me with a side-eye.

"Ugh, this child, god, have mercy... I did not," he replied and started walking towards the table.

"Why were you even with her?" I ran behind him.

"I can't tell you all that; I barely know you, and on top of that, you are supposedly in love with my best friend, so clearly, your loyalty is with him," he said with frustration.

"Yes, I like Yohanne, but that doesn't mean I will go and tell him... is it related to him?" I asked.

"No, it's not... it's not related to him, and now you've bored me so much, I give you 5 mins to chill and miss Yohanne; then we start something good or else I drop you back," he said and then pulled his bag from the chair.

"What are you doing for 5 mins while I think and miss Yohanne?" I asked, giving him a sarcastic smile.

"I'll miss the one I love, and this," he took a box of cigarettes out of his bag.

"So you do love someone... who is it, you have to tell me," my eyes could pop out in shock.

"I can't tell you," he said and started walking outside.

"You absolutely can," I started walking fast to match my pace with him.

"It was something strong, like a string pulling me in," he said while opening the café door. We stepped outside.

"Oh, romantic," I giggled, and he smiled too. "I hate you," he said, giving me a side-eye again.

"Okay then," I pushed him with my shoulder. I was so happy for him.

"I just wanted to talk and help..." he stopped and looked at me.

"Where is she now? You're just giving me bits and pieces," I said.

"Then it's your job to put these pieces together, not mine," he lit the cigarette.

"No, they are your pieces; you put them together," I said, and he laughed and threw his arm at me and pulled me in for a hug, his tall body was really heavy on my shoulders, but I managed. His pink sweatshirt was so soft; that hug felt like hugging a bear.

"Listen, Yohanne misses his mom a lot; maybe you getting the picture as a gift might ignite something," he said.

"I will! Thanks for the suggestion

I went back home and decided to get my guy a gift he would love.

"Mommmmm, I need you to call your new boyfriend," I yelled across the living room, looking for my mom. "Come up, I'm watching TV," she yells back. I walked the stairs and jumped on the couch next to her. A quick glance at the balcony with a smile, and then back to mom.

"So..." mom interrupted me mid-sentence. "What new boyfriend?" she asked, raising her eyebrows.

"I said I need you to call my new boyfriend's dad," I smiled, hoping she would not catch me. She smiled back and grabbed her phone from the table. "I'll call him, but what do you want me to tell him?" she asked me, dialing his number.

"Please ask him to help me get Yohanne's childhood picture with his mom," I said, looking at her phone, expecting her to do that right away. "I don't think it's a good idea, Aalu," she said with concern in her voice. "At least ask," I requested. "Okay, only for you," she clicked on the call icon, and the phone started ringing.

The ringing ended, but he didn't answer the call. "Should we try again?" I asked her; she nodded. The phone started ringing again, but he did not pick.

Her face looked sad. I asked myself if there's a slightest possibility that she really liked him. I wanted to ask her, but I did not. Maybe she needed more time to accept.

"It's 7 pm; he must've left the clinic. But go check if you see his car?" she said. I immediately got up and ran to the balcony. "No, mom, his car is not there." "I'll ask for him later," she said and unmuted the TV, drowning herself into the show. I could see her going deep into her thoughts. The expressions were still.

I turned back and saw Yohanne standing on the balcony. I raised my arm with a smile, gesturing him to hold it. He did the same, but his smile seemed different; his eyes were looking at me. We stood there looking at each other. He waved at me and went inside. I looked down when I saw his dad's car coming from the left.

"Mom, his dad is here. Can you please go and talk to him?" I requested her. I didn't know why I was doing that. I just wanted her to feel safe and talk to him. She hesitated a little and got up. I saw her walking down. I wanted to follow her, but I did not. I went to the balcony and saw Yash coming out of his car. He looked towards our gate and smiled; I could not see mom from this angle. He looked up at me and waved at me; I waved back with a smile. He walked towards her when I saw my dad's car moving towards the house. My heart sank.

CHAPTER 14

Shraddha

"He was standing in front of me, he looked up and waved at Ahilya. He walked towards me and stopped at a distance. 'Hi...!' he said, looking at me. "Hi...? I thought you were my friend..." I said. "I am." "Friends pick up calls," I complained, looking at him without blinking. He came a little closer. "I'm sorry I could not, how can I make up for it?" he asked. I saw Zaid's car moving towards us; I looked at him, and like a wife, I opened the door for him, and he got his car inside the yard to park it.

He took the car inside, he looked at me and Yash, and then turned his eyes back on the steering wheel. "I need Yohanne's childhood pictures, especially with his mom for his birthday," Ahilya said, jumping into the conversation.

"Yes, this is why I was calling you," I said and smiled. "Beta, you take them; I'll go check on Dad. Please help her out, Yash." I said and walked back inside. I did not turn back to look at him; I couldn't. I walked inside and saw Zaid standing there, near the dining table. "I'm really tired," he said, moving towards me; he hugged me, he did what I wanted for a long time but it was too late. He got too late. I hugged him back gently; I didn't want to hug him.

"What happened, Zaid?" I asked, pushing him slowly enough for him to not realize. "I don't know, Shraddha," he said, almost in tears. "It will all be alright," I said patting his shoulders and back slowly.

"I saw you walking with him yesterday, I saw you really happy and..." he said. My heart stopped, my blood went cold, and I could not breathe. "And...?" I asked him, trying to keep my cool. "Do you want to leave me?" he asked, and my senses were blocked; I stood still, looking at him, wondering how could he manage to collect the strength to ask me that question. I didn't think about the answer or the outcome, like the answer to that question was ingrained in every part of my body.

"No, I don't want to leave you," I said. How could I leave him, after all these years. "I love you," he hugged me again so tightly. "It's okay; relax now, go freshen up, and I'll cook something," I said and moved towards the kitchen, avoiding eye contact with him.

I could sense his eyes on me. He took his bag and walked away. I placed my hands on the kitchen platform, and a tear rolled down my face. I started crying; I was feeling after years, I had kept everything, every emotion deep inside of my heart. I cried for the times I needed him and he wasn't there, how we lived together for years without love. "Why didn't you leave, Shraddha? Why didn't you leave?" I wanted to throw things, but I couldn't. I had to stay calm. I closed my eyes and saw Zaid's face, how he asked me to marry him and I said yes.

That night,

I opened my eyes and looked at the ceiling; I took a deep breath. It was midnight, and I could not fall asleep. I kept looking at the ceiling. Nothing was changed; I was still sleeping next to my husband. I turned my head towards him; he had his eyes closed, but his body was restless, he kept moving.

I turned to him and placed my hand on his shoulder. He opened his eyes and looked at me. We both were looking at each other without saying a word. He took my hand and held it tight; he shifted a little towards me, I stayed put. He came closer and kissed me on my cheeks and on my forehead. "You can talk to me," he said, looking into my eyes. Tears started to fill my eyes, and one fell on my cheeks; he gently wiped it. "I know I wasn't there for you emotionally; I'm sorry I kept you away for so long. But I do love you, and I made a mistake, Shraddha," he said, placing his palm on my cheek. "Do you love me?" he asked; I looked at him. "I don't know, Zaid, I haven't felt this feeling for a while, and it feels so new," I got up and sat straight, he got up and sat next to me. He held my face into his palms. "You can tell me. It's me," he said, and I couldn't stop myself from hugging him. I hugged him as tight as I could.

"I'm sorry I don't know what I want, Zaid. I'm so lost, and I can't be lost; I have to be there for you and for Aalu; she looks up to me, and I can't do this to her," I said, crying in his arms. He held me tight; I could hear his heartbeat getting faster. "Listen... listen," he pushed my shoulders with his hands to be able to look at my face. "Would you want Ahilya to do something against her will? No, right, you gotta do what your heart says," he said with tears in his eyes.

"Are you crazy? What are you asking me to do?" I stood up from the bed. "I'm asking you to pick your happiness, and I know, I know you are not happy like this with me," he said; he stood up and held me by my shoulders. I was speechless; when it was his turn to fight for this relationship, he was letting me go. "You're letting me go? Without fighting for me?" I asked him; I was mad at him for not at least trying for me. He said nothing and kept looking at me; our faces were wet with tears. "Is it that easy for you to just let me go?" I asked, hoping that it would break his silence.

"It's not... it's the toughest thing I have to go through, but I'm not able to keep you happy, and I love you so much," he fell on his knees. "Then make me happy; it was never so hard? Be worthy of me, Zaid... at least try," I yelled on the top of my lungs. "At least try," I fell on my knees crying. "I failed, Shraddha; I'm sorry," he said and stood up and walked away. I stayed on the floor crying, remembering when we got married. When I first saw him, he was standing by his car looking at me and his friends, he smiled at me, and I knew I loved him. I knew something strong, something unbreakable was building. We both knew we were not meant for each other. We both fell in love that afternoon when I first took his hand in mine, pretending to read his palm, and he came so close to me.

I cried thinking how could he just give up on me like this. I collected myself and sat on the bed. I walked out of my room and saw a shadow on the balcony; I ran to see if Zaid was standing there. As I slid the balcony door, I saw Ahilya sobbing in the dark. I immediately hugged her. "What happened? Why are you crying?" I asked her, holding her tight. "You don't love Dad, right?" she asked, "I heard you guys fight, and it's okay, Mom, it's okay if you have to pick yourself before us; I'm there with you." She said, "Calm down, Aalu; I'm not leaving you guys, I'm not." I grabbed her by her shoulders; I didn't want her to think our family was getting apart. I hugged her, "Calm down first, please." I held her until I could feel her breaths getting back to normal. "My sweet baby," I said. "You love Yohanne's dad, right?" she asked. I looked towards his house, "No, Ahilya, I don't love him. Come, let us sit down." I made her sit on a little step at the balcony entrance. "Relax now and listen to me; me and Dad are not separating," I said. "I know, but I think you should," she said. I was shocked listening to this, as all my life I felt that we were the ideal couple for my daughter."

"Why do you want us to break up?" I asked in sheer confusion. "You don't love each other, Mom. I've never seen you guys in love," she said, her tears coming back up. "No, no, no crying again," I consoled her and took her hand in mine. We sat on the balcony looking at the sky trying to calm down. And the memories started hitting me. She rested her head on my shoulder for a few minutes.

"I was only 22 years old when I saw him for the first time; I felt an instant connection towards him. I knew I could even die for him, but our castes were different. Being a Hindu girl, I could never marry a Muslim guy." "Were you racist too?" she asked. Of course, I was not. "No, I was not racist. But my family was. Our second meeting is when I realized I had fallen in love with him. It was our friend's birthday, and we were all chilling on an empty road. It was windy, and he just stood there afar, looking at me. I looked at him, and I just knew that I will never ever love anyone how I love him. I had to fight everyone just to reach him. Nani even slapped me once when I lied and sneaked out to meet him," I giggled, remembering that slap and how worth it was.

"Why are you laughing remembering that slap?" she asked with a confused look. "Okay, so I had fallen in love with your dad, but he did not fall so quickly. The day I sneaked out, he was in Delhi with his friends, and I had to pretend that I'm coming to meet his friends. Somehow his friends left us alone, and we were together. I didn't know what to do, so I told him I could do palm reading, and he gave me his palm to read. I held it for the first time, and, well, after that day, actually after a year of that, I got to know that he fell in love with me during that palm reading." I said, my tears were all dried up, and there was a smile on my face.

"This is not mentioned in the book?" she asked. "Because this is my side of the story, Aalu, not his," I replied. "I will not give it all up so easily." I assured her. I felt a sense of relief, narrating my story to our daughter felt like a burden was taken off my chest. I was ready to sleep and wake up to a new beginning.

"Are you sleepy, Mom?" she asked, and I was very sleepy. "Yes, I am. Are you not?" I asked her. "No, Mom, I'm not, but it's not important. You please go to bed; I'll sit here for a while and sleep soon." She said smiling. I was relieved looking at her smile. I got up and walked towards my room; Zaid was fast asleep. I laid next to him and closed my eyes. I was filled with positive energies; I was dreaming of our time.

I woke up a little later than usual; I turned to Zaid, but he wasn't there on his side. I got up from the bed to check in the washroom. The door was open, and he wasn't there. My happiness faded slowly. His bag was not there either. I went back to the bed and picked up my phone from the side table. I dialed Zaid's number and called him. The phone started to ring, and he picked.

"Hello, Shraddha, aaj jaldi jana tha, and tum so rahi thi, so I left." He said and hung up the call before I could say anything. I dialed him again, but he didn't pick up. I walked out of my bedroom; I looked around, and my mind was blank. I saw the sofa in the living room; I walked towards it and sat on it. I slowly fell on my right and buried my face into the sofa.

I could hear some noises from Ahilya's room. I collected myself and went to check on her. As I opened her door, she was there painting something, with full concentration. "What's that?" I asked; she suddenly came out of her trance-like state. "Huh? Mum, you're up!" she smiled at me and slowly turned the canvas towards me.

I saw a beautiful half-painted portrait of Yohanne. "Wow! You really like him, don't you?" I asked her, as I had never seen such perfection in any of her paintings. "It's him, Mom. I've never felt this way for anyone." She said, I could see the same love in her eyes that I had years back.

"What's the problem then?" I said leaning on her door. As I knew this conversation will be a long one, yet I didn't want to barge into her room and distract her. "Hmm, the problem... I don't think he loves me back." She said; she kept her paintbrush on the table and looked at me, expecting me to solve her problems.

"Why do you think he doesn't? Did you ever ask him?" I asked her. "No, I never asked him, and we couldn't even spend more time after my realization." She said. "When was this realization?" I asked. "You remember I got my periods? That day when we were dancing, I found myself so much at peace and so happy. I just saw him, and I just fell for him." She said; there was confusion on her face.

"Finish your painting; I'll make breakfast for us." I left her alone with her thoughts, as everyone needs it at times. I went down to the kitchen to make something for me and Ahilya. The doorbell rang, and I had to go out to check who it was. I tucked my hair behind my ears; I felt uncomfortable attending to the door in a nightgown but I had no choice. I unlocked the door and pulled it.

I saw Yash standing in front of me with a photo album. "Hi, you had asked for it, so I thought I will give it to Ahilya," he said. There was a sense of awkwardness between us. "Please come in; I'll call Ahilya... Ahilyaaa come down." I called out to Ahilya. He entered the house and sat on the couch in the living room.

"Water? Or maybe breakfast?" I asked, and he smiled and looked down. "No, I'm good, thank you," he said. Ahilya walked down the stairs and looked at me standing with Yash; I felt an urgent need to tell her that he came by himself, and I did not call him.

"He is here with the album you asked for; have a look." I said, asking her to sit with him. "Oh, hi uncle, thanks for getting it." She came and sat near him on the sofa. He handed her the album and opened it with a smile. There was a picture of Yohanne where he was an infant. "Oh my god, look at him, so small." She giggled, looking at that and passed it towards me. I took the photo and looked at it. "Cute," I said. He smiled at me.

She saw the next picture, which was a photo of Yash and Divya holding Yohanne, face towards each other looking in the eyes. "You guys look so in love." Ahilya said and suddenly looked at my face. I passed her a smile. She started turning the photos on the Album when she found a picture of Yohanne and her mom. "I'll take this one." She said and pulled the picture out from the album.

"I will go and get it laminated and framed, Mom; I'll be right back." She said and ran upstairs to take her bag. I sat on the couch looking at Yash. "I'm really sorry I did that; I'm in love with my husband, but I had just lost myself at that moment." I said, avoiding eye contact.

"Hey, hey, hey, it's okay; you don't have to feel bad about anything. I still respect you the same." He said and moved towards me; he sat on the floor on his knees and grabbed my hand. I looked at him and took my hand off his grip. "Can you please sit up? If Ahilya sees you, she will think otherwise." I said, and he got up. "I'm really sorry." He sat next to me for a second and then stood up.

"I should get going." He took the album from the table and started to walk towards the main door. I waited for him to turn back as I wanted to look at his face once. I wanted to stop him, but I knew that would be wrong. I saw him walking out of the main door.

CHAPTER 15

Yohanne

"I'd been stalking Ahilya on Instagram, but I could not meet her for the past 4 days. I saw her photos with Sumair on her Insta-story. She tried reaching out, but I avoided. She even showed up, but I told her I wasn't feeling well, so I won't be able to hang out with them. We did come across each other on the balcony. The more I avoided her, the more I missed her. I could see a sense of sadness on her face for the past few days. I don't know what it is. Help me if you can," I had sent a voice note to my mom. I had done this multiple times in the past but never got any reply from her. I sighed and leaned back on my bed; it was 11 pm, and I had to go meet Sumair. I didn't want to, but it was my birthday, and I can't just leave the friendship solely because he got the girl I wanted. I got up and convinced myself to get ready. I pulled the black shirt from the cupboard but didn't want to wear that. I kept it back inside and pulled a white shirt. I got ready and looked at my reflection in the mirror. I walked down and found my dad sitting in the living room.

"Can you wait for a while?" he asked, and I ignored, I kept walking. "Please, Yohanne?" he said again and walked towards me, he stood at a distance. Something happened inside. I stopped. "What do you wanna say?" I asked him, still facing the door. "I know you have plans, and you wanna go out but 5 mins?" he asked, and I turned back. I looked at him, and my heart was not filled with hatred. "Come," he said and walked towards the sofa. There was a box kept on the table.

I sat next to him, and he grabbed the box. He pulled out a picture of me when I was born. "See, this is the picture your mom had sent me of you when you were born," he showed it to me. "And you decided to take me from her forever?" I questioned. "You still think I did that?" "Yeahhh!" "Well, I loved you and still love you more than anything in this world, Yohanne, but I can assure you I did not steal you from your mother." He said. "I don't wanna talk about it " I said and avoided looking towards him. His phone rang, and he hung up. "Pick it!" I said. "It's okay, the call can wait; my son shouldn't." he said and smiled. The phone rang again, and he turned his phone on silent. "It's okay, pick it," I said. He took the call and stood up. I kept looking at him. "It's just one patient who is having heartaches," he said, making it sound so casual. "I think you should go and check; if it's a heart attack and if he dies, how will you live with another guilt?" I said, and we both stayed still. I stood up to leave. "Umm okay and happy birthday, Yohanne." He said and came forward for a hug. He hugged me without my permission, and I couldn't stop him or push him. He looked at me with a smile and walked away.

A few minutes later I walked out of my house and found a red shiny gift box. I opened it, and there was a small frame which had a picture of me and mom on it. A smile appeared on my face remembering the beautiful time I had when she was just my mother. The memory got interrupted with the vision of me being dragged. A tear rolled down my cheeks. I could hear my screams; I was calling my mom, I had a red birthday cap on, and they just dragged me out. My breath started getting heavy, and I felt uneasy. I walked outside to get some air. I kept walking, but the flashes got out of hand. I found a bench ahead near the park and could see a man sitting there. I walked up to the bench and sat there. I broke into tears. A hand patted my back; I turned to see, and it was Ahilya's Dad.

"Are you okay?" he asked. I controlled my emotions looking at him and wiped my tears. "Hmm yeah, I am, thank you." I tried to put a smile on my face. "It will all be alright son," he kept his hand on my shoulders. "I keep losing the people I love." I said, wasn't sure if I was making the right decision opening up to him. He looked at me. "My mom left me when I was a kid." I said looking at him. "She didn't leave me actually; my dad forcefully took my sole custody." He laughed and looked away. "Looks like your dad has a habit of taking over people who belong to others." He said, and I knew what he was suggesting at. "I hated him all my life, but today..." I said and stopped "Today you forgave him? Today you feel you are healed?" he asked, and I was shocked how did he know what I was feeling. "Maybe, but I don't want to, and I don't know why I'm feeling bad for how I have been living." I said, he patiently heard me. "I've been doing things to hurt him, to hurt myself, you know, I've been a rebel, and now it feels like..." "The time has gone?" "How do you know what I'm about to say?" "I don't know kid; I guess I'm a man with a similar life.." he said. "Will I stop loving her too?" I said, joining the dots I took a pause and continued. "What's the point though; I think I've lost her already." "Who?" he asked, and I knew I could not tell him tell. "It's just a girl I really love." I said wiping the tears off my face. "Hmm, I just hope it's not my daughter." He laughed, and I kept quiet. "Why are you sitting here so late?" I asked him looking at the time. It was 11:45 pm. "Just like that, it's a beautiful night." He said and looked at the moon. "Thanks." I said and smiled at him. "Anytime, you can talk to me if there's something you can't tell your dad." He said and got up. I smiled at him. He started walking ahead, and I stood there looking at the moon. My phone rang, and it was...

CHAPTER 16

Ahilya

"How is it looking?" I asked Sumair, placing the portrait on the stage. I was so proud of myself for creating such a beautiful painting of him.

"Ehh, it looks average," he said, fixing the mic on the stage.

"He will come from there, and in about 10 minutes, the band will come with our gang," he said, looking at his watch. "I'm excited," he said, and I gave him a happy glance. "I can't wait for him to come," I said, and we sat on the stage looking at the balloons and the lights. "These lights are so pretty. How old is he turning?" I asked.

"24 years," he said, looking at the door. "You do so much for your friends," I said and turned my face towards him.

"No, I don't. It's just Yohanne," he said, a subtle smile on his face as he took his name. "Because he is your best friend?" I asked. He looked at me without uttering a word. Suddenly the door opened, and we saw a small band with a guitarist and a guy with a flute coming in. Sumair jumped from the stage and walked towards them.

"Hey guys, come in, you gotta set up on that stage," he directed them towards the stage and saw me looking at him. I couldn't take my eyes off him. I wasn't sure if what I was thinking was right or not. I got off the stage and saw a group of people of my age entering. Sumair came to me.

"Come, I'll introduce you to our friends." I went to their table with Sumair.

"Hi guys, this is Ahilya, Yohanne's girlfriend," he looked at me and winked with a smile. My eyes were wide open with the mini shock he gave me. I smiled and waved at them. "Hi guys."

"So where did you guys meet?" a girl from the group asked.

"She is Richa, by the way," Sumair clarified. I held my hand out for a handshake. I shook hands with almost everyone without being able to keep their names in my head.

"Let me tell you, Richa, how they met. She is his new neighbor, and look at her, how cute she is, our boy just fell in love with her," he said smiling at me. I looked at them, and they were all in awe.

"It's 11:48 guys, did Yohanne leave from his place?" Richa said, and I looked at Sumair because I was not allowed to make any calls.

"I'll call him, and I'll be back," Sumair said and moved to a corner. My eyes were still on Sumair; I saw him trying to reach Yohanne, but it seemed like he would not pick up the call. I panicked a little; I knew he wasn't doing well and also that he had been ignoring me for a few days. I took a deep breath and waited.

An hour later, "I guess he is not coming, guys. We should get going," a guy from the group said. I was getting tired too; my back started to ache a little.

"It's alright, guys. I'm not able to reach Yohanne; you guys carry on. I will wait," Sumair said. Slowly everyone started taking their bags and leaving us two.

"I think we should just go and check at his place," I said, looking at the time. I knew he would be at home, and also it was getting too late.

"Yeah, makes sense," he said and got up from his place. He lent me a hand to help me get up. "Should I get the painting too?" I asked him. "It's too heavy, Ahilya; we will show it to him tomorrow," he said. "Hmm, you're right."

We moved out of the café, and he turned off all the lights. We reached the society; I got out of the car even before the car could stop. I saw the main door wasn't locked; I turned to look if Yohanne's car was there. It wasn't. I had no hope; my heart kept saying that he had run away, far from me. Sumair followed me and looked at me; without saying a word, he understood everything. I sat on the stair which led to the main door of his house.

"Where is he, Sumair? Why has he been avoiding me?" I buried my face in my palm; he sat next to me and didn't say anything. We both kept looking at the road, hoping he would appear.

"He is at war, Ahilya," suddenly Sumair broke his silence.

"Aren't you?" I asked him; he looked at me. "So are you, little girl; we all are at war," he said, trying to hide his tears. He looked up at the moon. "My war is with myself, my war is with my love," he said.

"Whom do you love?" I asked. "Look at the moon," he said, pointing at the moon. I turned my head up to look at it; it looked extremely beautiful. It wasn't even a full moon that night; it was just a thin line of light, like a nose ring on a beautiful girl. I smiled.

"You know what's so beautiful about the moon and why it's so satisfying being in love with it?" He asked.

"Why?" I replied, intrigued to know what he had to say.

"You love it knowing that you can never reach it; you can never fully have it. But it will come to see you every day, and you are allowed to love him as much as you have in yourself."

"Hmm, you can love him," I said; I had noticed how it became him. I knew the moon wasn't just the moon for him; he was someone else. Whom he could only see but never reach.

"Why didn't you ever tell him?" I asked. "How could I? He would be disgusted of me. Now, at least I get to meet him every day; I get to be in love with him every day; no one can ever force me to stop loving him," he said. I understood that day that Yohanne was just a guy I was attracted to and felt happy with, but he was Sumair's everything.

"Were you jealous when I told you I loved him?" I asked. I was so close to Sumair; it felt like he was my only friend, and after knowing his truth, I just could not lose him as a friend.

"Oh, I hated you so much, but then I knew that Yohanne was straight and he will never be my boyfriend, so I had to convince myself that you would be the right choice," he said with a smile on his face.

"You are one of the purest, most sweetest persons I've ever known," I said, leaning my head on his shoulder and wrapping him with my arms.

"And you are my sautan... but okay," we both laughed at it. "I miss Yohanne, and I hope he comes back," I said, taking a deep breath.

CHAPTER - 17

2 Years later

Yohanne

"I was sitting on this bench with her dad, I got a call, and it was from the hospital. They said my dad was in a car accident, and I was rushed to the hospital. He had lost a lot of blood, and they said they couldn't save him," I said, gasping for breath. I was sitting in a cold white room on a grey couch in front of a tea table and a white lady.

"I'm so sorry for your loss," she said with pity in her eyes. I looked at the time, and it was running. I had a lot to say; I had paid a lot for these 50 minutes. I just wanted it all to come out, and she could fix it and give me back.

"Can we not talk about this again?" I asked.

"Yes, but Yohanne, you need to release this. We have one more session, and you haven't opened up about this much," she said gently.

"I kept blaming him all my life, without knowing that it was my mom who left him, and she never chose me while he kept choosing me every day. And I—" I couldn't keep my tears in any longer.

"I just insulted him, and now he is gone," I sobbed on her couch; she kept looking at me with sympathy. I stopped and wiped my tears; I was not gonna let this lady get a show.

"It's okay, Yohanne, you gotta let it out," she said. The time was running out, and she didn't even have an extra minute for me.

"I want you to write to your dad," she said, writing something down on her tab as well.

"You did not get it? He is not alive," I yelled.

"I know, but since there's a lot you gotta tell him, right? You miss him. So, I want you to start writing to him and tell him everything you could not," she said. There was a heaviness in my throat making it difficult for me to gulp.

"Hmm, okay... thanks, doc," I stood up. I could barely smile at her.

"I will see you next week, and if you feel comfortable, you can read one of the pages to me where you talked to your dad," she said. I didn't pay much attention to that and walked out the door. Visiting her was the toughest thing I had to do this year.

The first thing would be finding a place to stay. I just could not stay at that house any longer. She had done a huge favor paying for my tuitions and my therapy; I didn't want her husband to also keep me under his roof and feed me.

I exited the building; it was snowing outside. I looked up at the beautiful blue sky of Canada. I covered my head with the hoodie before stepping on the road. I kept walking and looking around for a store where I could get a book. I started observing people. How they hide their feelings so beautifully. I just didn't understand what had happened to me.

I stopped by one store which had a Christmas theme painted on the glass. I didn't pay much attention to it and pushed the glass door. I looked for a notebook section.

"Can I help you?" I turned to look towards the sweet voice. It was a girl with brown hair, white skin, and pink beautiful lips.

"Hey, yes sure, I'm just looking for a notebook," I said, I had a little smile on my face.

"Follow me, please," she said and started walking ahead. I followed her. "Here," she said, grabbing a book from the last shelf. "I'm sure you'll need a pen with it too," she asked.

And she wasn't wrong, I did. I just smiled and nodded. She picked up and kept it on my book and passed it to me. "Thanks," I said, "Carol," she replied, giving me her name. "Thanks, Carol," I said, and she blushed.

I paid for the book and the pen and gave her a smile before leaving the store. "I wish you were her," I mumbled and started walking again in the snow. The streets were beautifully covered with snow and lights.

I entered my building; it was an old one with only 10 floors in it. That's all I could afford. I lived on the second floor, which is why I never had to use the elevator. I walked the long white corridor of the 2nd floor to reach my apartment. I unlocked my door; my roommate worked in the morning, so he would only come in to sleep. The apartment wasn't big; it had an open kitchen and one bathroom. There were two single beds adjacent to each other against the walls with desks next to each bed.

I threw my bag on the bed and laid back on it. I closed my eyes and missed my life back in Pune. "Why did you come here?" I said to myself. I got up and pulled my bag. I unzipped it and took out the new notebook I had bought.

I took the pen, and the first thing I did was write my name on the first page. "Yohanne Yash Sharma." I had so much to tell him but nothing to write. I took a deep breath and started writing.

Hi Dad!

Yohanne here, your only child who was a disappointment.

You must be laughing at me, right? You kept me like a king, and here I'm washing my clothes, cooking shit, and trying to survive. I'm sorry I misunderstood you all my life, and I don't know how to fix this. I'm just hoping that whatever I write here is reaching you.

You know when I heard about your accident, I had tears in my eyes, and I was so confused about that emotion. I didn't know I loved you so much, but by the time I realized, you were just gone. Can you come back? Can you at least give me a dream? I just want to hug you once, I wanna hug you just once and hear you call my name. And then I will allow you to go, but I do want my childhood back. I want that time when I fell off the cycle, and you came to hold me, and I ran away.. I want that back. I will not run away this time. I will eat everything you'll cook for me, and I will be a good son, I promise. I don't want all this, I can trade everything that I have for just one last meet with you. I have so much to tell you, I have my whole childhood to share with you, how am I suppose to share it all in this book? When I don't even know if its reaching you or not.

Just come back.

Just come back.

The paper was drenched in my tears when I stopped writing. "Oh god, what a torture.. what a torture." I kept the pen in the book and closed it. I laid back on the bed looking at the ceiling, trying to distract myself from all my thoughts. My eyes got heavy, and I fell asleep.

I woke up to my phone ringing. I grabbed it and looked at the screen. Two years back, I would have died of happiness looking at the name on the screen; it said Mom. I picked up the call.

"Hi baby," she said. I didn't want to talk to her. "Hi mom," I said in a dull voice.

"It's your birthday tomorrow, baby! You wanna come home? Me and Dave are hosting dinner," she asked.

"I don't know, mom; my birthdays aren't very lucky for me, I feel," I said. I no longer felt the connection with her, and on top of that, my birthdays always reminded me of how my dad died in front of my eyes.

"It's just a dinner, love. Dave also wants to talk about some things," she said. I knew what he wanted to talk about. He wanted me to open my dad's fixed deposit and return them the money they helped me with on my MBA.

"I will ask Sumair to help me get the money for now," I said.

"No, it's not about money, it's just that we are concerned about your future. You're done with your MBA now, what's the plan ahead and all that. Please do come, and you will be there; then I can convince them to celebrate Diwali," she requested.

"I never liked Diwali anyway, but okay, I'll think."

I threw the phone aside and got up, I walked a little around my apartment. I ate a few biscuits, had some water. I kept my phone on charge. I had no TV in my apartment, so the phone was my only source of entertainment.

It was 7 pm, I missed Sumair… and I missed Ahilya too. "Ahilya." I misunderstood her, I misunderstood my dad, and I didn't know my own best friend. I checked my phone's battery; it was still 20 percent. I left it there and left the apartment; my room mate would come any time, tired, and I just didn't want to listen to him talk about his tiring day.

I locked the apartment behind me and walked down the stairs. The streets were beautiful, and the cold would just numb my thoughts. The coldness hit my nose and cheeks. I walked on the streets looking at people, some were there with their families, some alone, some without a home, sitting on the footpath. I wished I had enough money to help them.

I kept walking; I could see the store from where I had bought the book. I saw the girl standing and giving away candies to kids. I walked up to her and stood next to her.

"Hi Charlotte!" I said smiling, being proud that I remembered her name.

She turned and gave me a wide smile. "Hi Dylan!" she said handing me a packed candy.

"My name is not Dylan," I said clearing her doubt.

"Oh, I thought we were calling each other with wrong names, but honestly, it's not my fault that you don't remember my name, and you were so rude that you didn't give me yours," she said.

"Oh, I'm really sorry, I'm Yohanne," I said, holding out my hand. She turned to me and smiled; she shook my hand.

"I'm Carol, not Charlotte." "I'm sorry Carol; I'll remember." I kept holding her hand. "I'm out of candies, kids; will see you tomorrow." She said and waved at the kids taking her hand away from my grip.

"Come, let's walk," she said. I was blushing, and I followed her.

"Thanks for letting me walk with you," I said, and she gave me a weird look.

"That's okay, why are you Indians like this? Always so awkward."

"Ah, I'm not awkward." I defended myself.

"You are, don't take offense; you're hot but awkward," she said and kept walking.

"Are you seeing anyone?" she asked me, I didn't have any answer to that.

"I'm not," I said. She stopped walking and turned to me.

"Even I'm not." She said and came closer to me. "Okay," I said and took a step back.

"Will you drop me home?" she asked slowly, holding my hands.

"Yeah, I will drop you home," I said, she grabbed my arm and pulled it. I followed her through those streets and lights. I was smiling and wasn't thinking much, she kept pulling my arm and I just followed her.

We stopped near a building, "this is me..." she smiled; she had a beautiful smile with beautiful lips.

She jumped and gave me a peck on my cheek and looked at me and waved slowly. She started walking towards her building. She turned a couple of times before getting in.

I stood there till she entered the building.

CHAPTER 18

Ahilya

"Did he pick up?" I asked Sumair, who was sitting on my bed in my Mumbai apartment with me at 10:30 am, hoping to reach Yohanne and wish him on his birthday.

"Nope, unreachable," he said. "So gaya hoga kya?" I asked him again.

"I don't know, Ahilya, maybe he is asleep, maybe he is on a date; all I know is he is not picking up my calls," he said in a frustrated tone.

"I'm sorry, I'll just wish him on Instagram," I said and took my phone.

"I'm sorry I got mad at you. I'm actually mad at him; he has completely changed since he went there, yaar," he said.

"I know he did. Maybe he found someone," I said, hoping that Sumair would tell me otherwise and calm my anxiety.

"Yes, I'm sure he is seeing someone, and it's high time you also move on and start going out with Rahil," he suggested. I got annoyed at each word that had come out of his mouth.

"I don't love Rahil, and I don't want to be his girlfriend, Sumair. If you can't understand such a simple thing, then I think you should not be my friend," I replied, getting up from my bed and walking towards the bathroom. I picked my phone from the table before entering the bathroom. "Where are you going?" he asked.

"Susu," I locked the door and sat on the toilet seat, annoyed and irritated by what he had said. I took a deep breath and unlocked my phone. I opened Instagram and clicked on Yohanne's chat. The last text I had sent him was a thank you when he wished me on my birthday. I started typing.

"Hi Yohanne, Happy Birthday! I hope you're doing well. We tried reaching you but couldn't. I miss you."

"Stop texting him from inside!" Sumair screamed from outside.

"I'm not!" I screamed back. "Susu doesn't take so long, Ahilya. I've been your best friend for 2 years; I know you," he screamed.

I opened the door. He was standing there right in front of me. "What?" I said with a neutral face. "What did you text him? Ohh..my prince, my love? Come back, your Juliette is waiting," he said, enacting Juliette.

"Go ahead, check," I handed him my phone.

"Hi Yohanne.. Happy birthday.. who will say baby Ahilya? I hope you're doing well; we tried reaching you but couldn't. I miss you, smiley.. awwww, that's so sweet," he said and hugged me.

"You really think he is seeing someone else?" I asked, biting my lips.

"Maybe he is. He posts nothing on social media, and he is hot. He might be," Sumair suggested.

"I really miss him, Sumair. How do I move on?" I said, dropping my head on his chest. He wrapped me in his arms. "Exactly what I felt when I thought he might be in love with you," he said, and I giggled.

"Now go out and wait, please. I have to get ready," I said, pushing Sumair out of the room. "Is there anything to eat?" he yelled from outside. "Check in the fridge, but I doubt kuch hoga. Mom is in a lot of stress, and I don't force her to cook," I yelled back. Mom had started working again, and I didn't want to be a burden on her.

I opened my cupboard to pick my outfit for the day. I sat in front of my cupboard, looking at the pile of clothes. "Why didn't he pick my call? Why didn't he reply?" I asked myself. I knew he never loved me, but there was something, a little connection. I sighed at my situation and looked at the pile of clothes again.

I pulled a black t-shirt by its sleeve, and the whole pile fell on me. I tried to stuff everything back into the cupboard; a white dress fell from it. I picked it up, and it took me back to that day when he had hugged me. That was the day when I did feel something between us, pain in his eyes and love in his touch... then what changed.

I managed to stuff all the clothes inside and kept the dress aside. I got into the bathroom and turned the shower on; the water fell on my body. I started missing him even more, missing his touch. I got out of the shower; I looked at my reflection in the mirror. I had never seen my face so dull. It felt like I had lost the war. I looked dead, but I had to be normal.

I got out of the bathroom and wore the dress. I took a look in the mirror, which was placed on my dressing table. I smiled looking at myself. I grabbed my phone from the table. I saw a notification on it from Yohanne. My body could feel alive again. I clicked on it.

YO: Thanks

I read the text and realized that no reply was better than this. "Who the fuck does he think he is?" I screamed on top of my lungs. I bashed the door open and saw Sumair stuffing chips into his mouth. "Who... the fuck... does he think... he is?" I repeated myself softly yet sarcastically.

"What happened?" Sumair said while chewing his chips. I unlocked my phone and showed him the screen. "Look!" I screamed.

"Whoa, okay, at least you got a thanks... he didn't even call me back," he said, trying to console me. "Ahh really? Last year near his birthday he said he misses me. Is he bipolar?" I yelled; my emotions were out of my control. I started walking from one side of the living room to another.

"That's not bipolar disorder, sweety. And why are you letting it affect you so bad? You guys didn't even date," he said and ate another chip.

"I know, but I really miss him, how do I move on?" I said, dropping on the sofa next to him. "Look, I might be wrong, but I feel you are in love with him," he said, I snatched the pack from his grip and took a chip out. "Hmm, wow, brand new information, what else you've got?" I put the chip in my mouth and started chewing.

"Hmm, but he isn't," he said, taking the pack back from my hand. "You did not have to attack me like that, Sumair," I said, trying not to take it so deep, although his words did damage my soul.

"I'm not joking, Ahilya. Yes, I will agree to it that I saw something in his eyes for you, but maybe it was just infatuation. And he is moving on," he said, wrapping me in his arms. "Come with me; I'm going to meet Ahaan," he said.

"How lucky you are, you got Ahaan replacing Yohanne," I said in a baby voice. "You are dumb, Ahilya. You are not seeing your guy, but never mind, let's go; my bae is waiting for me," Sumair got up from the sofa, letting me fall on the couch. "Sure, let's go. Mom will come by evening, and I need to refresh my mind again before I start with my work," I got up from the sofa and pulled my shoes from the shoe rack.

"Nike! Yohanne loved Nike shoes," he said. I stood up and looked him dead in the eyes. I picked my other shoe and threw it at him. "Yohanne likes Nike, my foot."

We reached the restaurant where we were supposed to meet Ahaan. Sumair and I got a table for three, but they assigned us a table for four. Sumair sat in front of me, and I was facing towards the entrance. Sumair started looking at the menu to order, and I was distracted by my own thoughts. The entrance door opened, and a guy entered with a big bouquet of roses; due to the direct sunlight, I could barely see his face. He came a little closer, and I recognized him. He looked at me and kept his index finger on his lips.

He stood right behind Sumair and closed his eyes with his left hand and gave him a peck on his cheek. Sumair guessed who it was, and he got up to hug him. "Aww, they are so beautiful," Sumair said, hugging him again. "They are not for you, love. They are for our third wheeling adopted daughter," Ahaan said and handed me the flowers. Sumair gave me a look, and I was shocked myself. I took the flowers, and the three of us broke into laughter.

We sat down, and Sumair ordered sangria for me and two beers for them. "So, I was telling Ahilya that it's high time, and she should just forget him," Sumair complained to Ahaan.

"I think he is right. If Yohanne doesn't care about you, then love, you should just—" before Ahaan could finish, Sumair interrupted, "Dump his ass."

"They are not dating for her to dump his ass," Ahaan said, looking at Sumair. "I know I just wanted to say this line," he laughed and gave me a high-five.

"Sumair yaar. You guys don't get it," I said, irritated because they all kept forcing me to forget someone I wasn't ready to forget.

"Okay, okay, take your time, think, but for now, just focus on your art show. You're very young, and I'm trusting you with a lot right now. You have to make us proud," Ahaan said. The waiter served us our drinks. Ahaan opened the beer can and passed it to Sumair; he opened his and raised it.

"Cheers, guys, to our daughter," Sumair said. He was finally in his true self. I looked at him and smiled, genuinely happy for him. "After Kajal and Abhishek shifted to Australia, I literally had no one, but I'm so grateful for this friendship," I said, taking a sip from my glass.

"So basically, you've always been a third wheel," Ahaan said. "Yeahhh," Sumair sighed. I took it as a joke and smiled. My phone rang, and I looked at the screen. It was Rahil. "It's Rahil," I said to them.

"Pick it up; he is a nice guy, pick it," Sumair insisted. I swiped it up to answer the call. "Hello?" I said.

"Hey, Ahilya, how is it going?" he said in an excited tone.

"Umm, how's what going?" I asked.

"Your artwork that you'll be exhibiting?" he replied.

"Oh, that," I said and stood up from my seat. I kept my palm on the speaker, blocking my voice. "I'll be back," I said to Sumair and Ahaan and walked outside the restaurant.

"Hey, Rahil, now say, I was actually out with Sumair and Ahaan," I said.

"Oh, that's great. I was just excited for your big day. How's aunty, by the way?" he asked.

"Mom is fine; she is helping me a lot with her inputs," I replied.

"Hmm okay, let me know if you're free this evening. We can meet and hang out maybe," he said, his voice and his words felt true.

"I'll let you know, Rahil, if I can make it or not," I said and didn't wait for him to say bye. I hung up the call.

I hugged Ahaan and Sumair at the gate of the restaurant, handing the roses to Sumair. "They are for you, and I feel so happy to say that they will always be for you," I said, smiling at them. They looked so happy and so in love with each other. I walked backward a little, looking at them, waved them goodbye, and started walking. I passed by many stores, some big with beautiful mannequins on display, some food stalls.

I walked, trying to relax my mind. "So what if he didn't love you back, Ahilya? It's alright; you don't have to forcefully push him out of your heart," I said to myself. I looked at the sky; the sun wasn't so harsh. I took out my earphones from my bag and played a song. I always saw myself as the main character, and this was my time to enjoy the pain that came with being the main character.

Suddenly, a water droplet fell on my forehead. "Rain in December, how unusual," I looked up and kept walking. The frequency of the drops increased, and it started to shower heavily. I ran under a shed and wiped my hands. I looked at the rain again something clicked inside me and decided to go in it. I stepped out and looked up again. I smiled at my life and started walking again. It reminded me of the day I was shifting to Pune, that beautiful rainy day. I didn't know how my life would just change after that.

The smell of wet mud brought memories flashing in front of my eyes. I reached home in 16 minutes and 4 replays of my song. I entered my apartment and disconnected my phone from the earphones. Mom was already home. I went to her room and found her on the bed looking at her phone with her reading glasses. I walked straight into her room and hugged her.

"Kya hua, why are you drenched? All good?" she asked.

"No, Mom, it's not all good. Yohanne didn't pick up my call, and then when I texted him, he replied with a thanks. It's raining in December, the climate is messed up, and Rahil wants to get back with me, but I'm not able to get over Yohanne. Can you believe all this is happening all at once?" I cried to her, hugging her tight to restore my happiness.

"Okay, but why are we letting it affect us? Didn't you tell me that you don't care if he loved or loves you back or not, you want to keep loving him?" she reminded me.

"I know I did, but one-sided shit is so painful. And on top of that, Sumair keeps telling me to date Rahil," I complained and looked at her.

"Hmm, but we don't like Rahil?" she asked.

"We like Rahil; we don't love Rahil," I clarified. She slowly pulled my head onto her lap.

"Hmm, we love Yohanne, who doesn't love us back, and we still want to keep loving him, right?" she asked.

"Right," I said.

"Do you think it is right? Do you think it will do any better for us? And don't you think we should change before we catch a cold?" she asked.

"I don't know all that, Mom; I don't want to change. Let me get sick," I said.

"Sometimes it's not worth staying, Allu, especially when you know it's not the same from the other side," she said, walking to the bathroom. She grabbed a towel and gave it to me.

"You wanna cook something with me?" I asked her.

"What do you wanna cook?" she asked.

"Anything that'll keep my mind occupied till I forget about him," I said, keeping my tone high so that I could sound excited, and she would not understand the real motive behind it.

She chuckled at my words. "We can bake a cake? Anyway, it's just the two of us with no rules," she exclaimed.

CHAPTER 19

Shraddha

I looked outside the window; the night sky looked beautiful, there was a pull, a calling. I went down the building to take a walk. It was around 11 pm. Although Mumbai is a city that never sleeps, the streets around the building were silent, as it wasn't near the main road. I stepped outside the building exit; a cold breeze embraced me. I wrapped myself with my arms and rubbed my shoulders. I looked up at the stars.

Looking at the stars always made me emotional as it felt like I'm searching for someone in this crowd of a million people. It's said that when people leave us, they become a star. How was I supposed to find him amongst so many of these stars? My vision got blurred with the tears filling my eyes up. I kept walking in circles around the building.

I saw a couple of people entering through the society gate. I lowered my eyes, trying to avoid eye contact. I had lost so much in the past few years, but did I even have it? Was it even mine to lose? I thought to myself. I wanted to be strong for Ahilya; a smile appeared on my face. She did not deserve this. She deserved to be loved by her father, by me, and by us together. She deserved to fall in love with a guy who loves her back and would do anything to keep her happy.

I knew she was keeping a lot to herself. I had seen the love in her eyes for Yohanne; she might not accept it, but she isn't letting him go from her heart. It's the most beautiful pain to keep a part of someone in your heart even when they are gone. That part gives us a will to continue. It helps us without even realizing it.

My phone rang, distracting me from my deep thoughts. I was holding it in my right palm. I checked it, and it read "ZAID." I picked it.

"Hello?" I said. "Hello! I'm sorry; did I disturb you?" he said, his voice calming to my ears as always. "Of course, you did; I was in my thoughts taking a little walk and you called," I said, taunting him. It was something we did a lot before getting married.

"Oh, I'm so sorry! What were you thinking about?" he asked. "It's too personal," I replied. "Hmmm, I get it. How's Ahilya?" he asked. "Why don't you ask her yourself? Give her a call tomorrow morning; now she is asleep," I said.

I was walking slowly, taking in every second of the conversation. We would barely call each other but were always available. "I don't think I should call her, Shraddha. I don't think she is okay with me," he said with a bit of hesitation in his voice. "Why do you think that?" I asked.

"Forget it; just wish her luck for her art exhibition," he said. "Don't tell me you won't attend it," I said. "No, I won't. I don't think she wants me there," he said in a dull tone.

"Why would you assume that?" I yelled; he got me frustrated. I knew Ahilya wanted him to attend. She just wanted him to try to be her dad instead of just being her father. "How's your work going?" he asked very calmly, as if it didn't matter. "Are you serious, Zaid? I'm telling you that your daughter wants you to come, and you are distracting from the topic," I was yelling at him again, without even realizing.

"Why are you getting mad at me, Shraddha? Why are you screaming?" he asked. "You don't know why I'm screaming? It's the only way to reach you, to make you understand that what you did all those years, isolating us, was not good. We needed you, and you were in your head the whole time," I was shouting, my blood was boiling at that moment.

"I was there for you; I worked for the family, and I did what a husband and a father does," he defended. "No, Zaid, you did not. A father and husband are supposed to love his family, not just earn for them. How could I not understand that I had lost you years back?" I cried.

"You took a step back too, didn't you? After Ahilya, you were the one who didn't want another child," he said angrily. "Because we were not in love, Zaid. I was just your wife, and we already had a daughter. I wanted to give my attention to her before having another child and leaving Ahilya to grow all by herself. And how would you know that; you don't have siblings," I said. My heartbeat was racing, and I took a deep breath to calm myself down. He heard my breaths getting heavy.

"Are you okay? Please calm down," he said, lowering his tone. "Hmm, I'll be fine; I can't talk to you right now, Zaid. I'll call you later," I said. "Okay, please take care, and... I'm sorry," he said. "Hmm, bye," I hung up the call. I took a couple of deep breaths. I touched my forehead to control myself from crying.

I looked up at the stars again, hoping that he is looking down at me. "Ahhh, calm down," I said to myself. I looked around to see if anyone saw me yelling on the phone. There was no one. I wanted to sit on the floor and continue to look at the stars.

"I know I didn't want you, and I didn't have the strength in me to tell you how I was feeling, but why did you have to go like that?" I asked, looking at the stars. The wind started to blow, and it got a little chilly. I didn't realize that my face was all wet with tears. I wiped my tears with my hands. I turned back towards the entrance and looked up one last time before entering.

CHAPTER 20

Yohanne.

Hi Dad!

Today I won't bore you with my sob story. Today, I'll bore you with something I should have shared earlier. I don't know how to tell you; it's all so complicated. But okay, here it is. I met a girl, Carol. I've seen her multiple times. We have gone out on a couple of dates, and she is cute, pretty, and she tries to be funny. She likes me, and I like her too, but it's very different than how it was with her. You know her; you've seen me with her. I wasn't even this mature to understand that what I was feeling at that point was love. I'm trying to forget her because I know I can't be with her; we can't be together. I wish I could ask you what Mom was for you. Was she your Carol, or was she your Ahilya? Because if she was your Ahilya, then I'm so sorry for what you were going through, and I made it worse for you. I'm trying not even to think about her, but I guess she wants to stay friends. How do I stay friends with someone I love? She texted on my birthday saying "I miss you." But how to tell her that I don't just miss her; I can't stop thinking about her even after two years. Just take it away from me, and yeah, I will continue to date Carol. And one more thing. I'm going to see Mom; I went there on my birthday, it was nice. Jai is sweet, and well, initially, he did not like me, but now I think we are getting closer. Things are weird here; no one lives with their family, and that's why Dave felt very uncomfortable living with me, so I moved. I've learned trading to earn a few dollars. That helps me with my expenses. Mom helps me with my tuition fees and therapy. I will return them the money as soon as I get a job. I don't want to touch the money you left me. I will probably save it to buy a house here. I don't know; I'm thinking too much but maybe with Carol.

I will see you soon.

I kept the pen down on my desk, "no tears this time," I said to myself and looked at my reflection on the window's glass. The city was cold. I had to travel 15 kilometers to visit Mom, and I needed strength to pretend to be okay and happy. Before that, I had to meet my new girlfriend, Carol.

I picked up my phone, which was charging. There was no main light in my room; it was dimly lit with the lamp on my desk. I looked at the screen, and there was a missed call from Sumair. I felt bad for not staying in touch that much. It was a shocker for me to know he was gay. He needed me when he was leaving his family as his mom wasn't ready to accept him. I was selfish; I just avoided him. Still, he tries to reach out. I took a deep breath and closed my eyes. Thinking about Sumair somehow took me back to Ahilya.

"Ahilya," I sighed. I looked at my screen and dialed Sumair. The phone rang, and he picked it at once.

"Yohannee Sharma, my so-called best friend! Kesa hai kutte!!" he said with excitement taking over his voice slowly. His voice made me teary and got a smile on my face as well. I spoke to him last, months back.

"I'm good! How are you, bro?" I said. "Bhai, accent mein baat karta hai abh.." he said, and it made me realize that I had picked an accent in 2 years in Canada. "I'm good, bro.. happy belated birthday, me and aalu tried to call, but I guess you were busy," he said. "Yeah, I was on a date," I said, I was blushing thinking about the date but realized he took her name. I didn't want to think about her; I was happily moving on. "OH MY MY. Who is this girl who got Yohannes heart," he said, it seemed a little different as he always had a manly tone. Now he was completely accepting himself and talking openly. He was himself for the first time. "Ahhh her name is Carol. She works at a store near my building, and yeah, we have been on a couple of dates, and she is really cute," I said, I was stammering a lot while talking to my best friend. I didn't want to talk to him like that. I wanted to be as open to him as he was to me. But there was a wall blocking me from reaching out to him. "Wow, I'm so happy for you!! I wanna see her picture. You don't post anything nowadays," he asked for a picture. "Umm, I don't have any now, but I will surely click one today!" I replied. "Theek hai! I will wait for you to respond on Instagram," he said. "Yeah, I will," I replied. I could see he was trying to connect, and I couldn't explain to him how badly I wanted that too, but I was so far away. "Do you miss Ahilya?" he asked, something I didn't want to hear or answer. "I have to go Sumair, Carol is waiting, and I'm already late," I said and hung up the call.

I locked my apartment and was leaving to see Carol. As I turned and saw Tayne standing behind me. "Where are you going? I don't see you anymore brother all good?" he asked, I didn't feel the need to answer him, I smiled. "Yes, all good, I'll get going; my girlfriend is waiting for me," I said and left. I had to pick Carol from her store. I walked out of the building. It was Christmas eve in 2 days, and I had to help Carol with the tree in her store. I didn't know that the store belonged to her Dad. Since I had to go to Mom's today, she agreed on doing this on 23rd itself.

It was cold, and my hands were freezing as I walked ahead. I rubbed my hands together and blew some air on them to keep them warm. I saw Carol, outside her shop, waiting for me. She looked at my directions and a smile appeared on her face. She ran towards me, wasn't a sprint but a cute jog. She hugged me the instance she reached me, and I wrapped her in my arms. There was a comforting warmth in that hug. I kept her in my arms and tightened the grip. She smelled like cocoa butter and strawberries. I buried my face into her neck; her hair was all over my face. "Hi Baby!" she said, pushing me away slowly; she had a beautiful smile on her face. "Hi!" I said overwhelmed with the storm of feelings inside of me.

"Where are you taking me today?" she asked, but I had no plans made. I didn't know where to take her; I just had a café in mind where we had gone a couple of times. "You wanna umm have a coffee?" I asked hoping not to disappoint her. "Umm... no, I wanna have hot chocolate. It's so chilly, and hot chocolate is way better than coffee." "Okay, done! Let's go!" I said showing her the way to move ahead and lead me. "Why don't you ever plan a date Yohanne," she said holding my hand and pulling me. She did that a lot. "You know Dad is really looking forward to meeting you and decorating the shop together," she said. "Me too!" I said, and she turned back to give me a smile.

We reached a new café after six to seven minutes of walking. The café had outdoor seating as well, and it was beautifully lit with yellow Christmas lights. They already had their tree in place. "Look, they already have their tree in place Yoh! It's Christmas eve tomorrow, and we have to fix the tree anyhow." She commanded. "Yess, yess, baby, yess, we will, I will be there now can we order?" I patted her hand which was wrapped around my arm.

I pulled a chair for her, and she settled onto it. I took a seat in front of her.

"How's your therapy going?" she asked, taking my hand in hers.

"Um, it's going fine," I replied. I didn't want to tell her that I missed one session because I had to go on a date with her. I felt better with her compared to therapy.

Therapy tortured me while she was healing me and my heart.

"We will have two hot chocolates," she placed the orders, and the waitress smiled at us. "You two look really cute together," she said.

"Thank you," Carol said, shrugging in a cute way. "I love this place; I've been here with my ex," she said.

"Oh, your ex!" What was I thinking? She never dated anyone?

"Yeah, he was my high school boyfriend; my dad didn't like him at all," she said, looking around at the lights and not paying much attention to the topic. "Why didn't he like him?" I asked, my curiosity increasing.

"Yohanne! I was in high school, and Dad was just being protective. Nothing else," she said, looking into my eyes.

"Oh, okay, forget it." I looked at her; she was already looking into my eyes. "Do you mind pulling your chair near me?" she asked. I pulled my chair nearer to her. "I'm here!" She leaned in and gave a small peck on my lips; her lips were extremely soft, and she had cherry lip balm applied. I grabbed her and kissed her; the time had stopped, and I could taste her lip balm. It was our first kiss, and I didn't know why she picked the time, but I loved it. I pulled back and looked at her; we both blushed, and she pointed her finger upwards. I looked above me, and there was mistletoe hanging. I smiled and kissed her once more. This time it was more passionate.

We stopped when the waitress interrupted us. We looked at her, and she giggled looking at me. Carol looked at me and laughed. "You have my lipstick all over your face." She grabbed a tissue and cleaned my lips. I took her in my arms and closed my eyes. A glimpse of Ahilya came into my head, and I shook it off my head. "Are you okay?" she asked.

"Yeah, yeah, completely," I replied. She looked into my eyes; her left palm was still on my neck; she slowly slid it down. Her hands were cold yet very soft. She picked her cup with both of her hands as the cup was hot. She took a sip and did a cute little dance moving her shoulders right to left. "Try it," she insisted; I took a sip too, it was subtly sweet but very smooth. "Do you like it?" she asked; I looked at her and nodded. "So, did you like anyone before meeting me?" She asked. The first thought that struck my head was of Ahilya.

"Yes, I did," I replied and took another sip. "Tell me more about her," she asked, she placed her head on her fist and looked at me. Her focus was now on me instead of the hot chocolate. "Hmm, okay, well, she was my neighbor, and I never told her I was in love with her, and then I came here. Two years later, I found you," I said, trying to end the topic as fast as possible. "Aww, you never got to tell her!" she made a puppy face and rubbed my back. "By the way, I told my best friend about you, and he wants to see you, so can we take a picture together?" I asked her. "Oh my god, are we making it official now?" She asked and laughed. I looked at her as I didn't have anything to say on that. "Hah, I'm just joking; chill, come let's take a picture." She came closer and leaned on my shoulder. The lights were beautiful. I clicked a couple of selfies on my phone. "Send it to me! I will make it my wallpaper!!" she said. I smiled and airdropped her those pictures instantly. Her face was lit; she typed something on my phone and showed me. She was posting the picture on her Instagram story. It said, "New beginnings" with a heart and a Christmas tree. "I'm tagging you," she said. "Okay!" I said. I got a notification in ten seconds. I decided to repost the story. I knew that Ahilya will see the picture. Maybe she will feel bad.

"Whatever, as if she it'll affect her," I said to myself. "What?" Carol asked. "Nothing, I'm just reposting the story," I replied. "Really!!" she almost jumped from her seat and threw her arms at me to hug me. "Okay, now let me post it," I said, pushing her hands off me. "Hmm, go on," she said and picked up her cup. She soon got busy in her hot chocolate and her phone. I was confused. The picture was there on my screen; I didn't know what Ahilya felt for me, but I knew that once she sees this, it will be over. She will start seeing me as someone's boyfriend. I started missing every second I had spent with her. Her laughter, her perfume, her hair. I missed her essence in my life, and I knew. One click and this essence will go forever. "It's not a big deal, Yohanne; it's just a picture," I said to myself and clicked on the "your story."

The story got posted. I looked up at Carol and took a deep breath. "It's done," I said; she looked up from her phone and smiled. It felt like it didn't matter to her much. "Mitchelle just replied, saying 'you're into Indians now,'" she said and giggled. She kept looking into her phone, and my heart kept pounding. I checked on my phone who all saw my story, looking for her name; I wanted to see her name but at the same time, I was scared of how she would feel after looking at the story.

CHAPTER 21

Ahilya

"Are you ready?" Rahil asked, rubbing my back with very little pressure. This was the day I had waited for forever. "I am." It was my time to showcase my art. I was sharing the exhibition with 6 other artists, and I had been allotted two walls. I had 8 paintings to exhibit. I turned to have one last look at my portraits.

The first white wall had 4 paintings and one in between; the main painting was the one made with multiple colors, mostly purple and orange. It was the painting of me and Yohanne but without our faces. Only I knew it was us. On the other wall, the main painting was the one I made for Yohanne on his birthday. The one I could never show him. The one I could never give him.

"I'm getting too emotional, Rahil," I said. "I don't want to cry, do something." I said again. He was silent, not saying a word. "Why aren't you saying anything?" I turned to my left to look at him, and his eyes were fixed on the entrance of the gallery. I turned back completely, and I was stunned. The tears were no longer in my control. They rolled down my face as I saw Dad walking in, talking to Sumair and Ahaan.

"I'm sorry, Ahilya. I promised him I wouldn't tell you," he said. I looked at him, almost sobbing. "I told you I didn't want to cry; it'll ruin my makeup," I said, and he hugged me. "You can wipe your tears on my shirt." He said, and without giving it a second thought, I wiped my tears with his white shirt and left my foundation stains on it. "Sorry," I apologized for his shirt. "It's okay, let's call it your final art for the day." He replied, and I laughed.

I looked at Dad; he was almost near me. I ran towards him, stopped right in front of him. "Congratulations!" he said. I was expecting him to let go of the rudeness and just be my dad for now. "Thank you, Papa." I said, he smiled, and I saw his eyes; it had love for me this time. He smiled, then he opened his arms, and I hugged him. I laid my head on his chest and realized what "feeling safe" meant. I felt sorry for the first time for insisting mom on leaving him. At that moment, I realized that I had failed in understanding them. I didn't know the baggage they carried.

"You met Mom?" I looked up at him and asked. "Umm, no, is she here?" he asked. I nodded. "Yes, she just went out to get me something to drink so that I can calm down." I said. I still didn't leave him; my head was on his chest, and I was getting comfortable. "Okay, are you feeling better now?" he asked. "Hmm, I am." I replied. "Okay, listen, come on now." I pulled back and looked at him. "Tell me who is that young boy?" Dad asked, pointing at Rahil.

"Oh him? That's my friend Rahil." I replied. "Okay, he better stay a friend." He said. I giggled. "Yes, Papa, he will." I held him by his hand and pushed him gently towards my wall. He looked closely at my paintings. "Why do I feel I've seen this guy somewhere?" he said, looking at Yohanne's painting. "Yes, you have." I said. The smile vanished from my face. "Allu yeh le, have this." Mom said from behind. She had a berry cooler in her hand. She looked up at me and Dad standing. Her speed decreased; her expressions changed. "Hi, Shraddha!" he said and gave her a gentle hug. "Hi, you said you wouldn't come." She asked him. "I realized I've been a bad father, and I had to make it up to her." He said, slowly letting her go.

I took my phone out to take a selfie. "Hey, no, don't use your phone, use my phone; your phone's camera isn't good." Sumair interrupted. "My phone's camera is bad?" I asked. "Yes, use mine." He said and took my phone from my hand. "Listen, let me click all the pictures and put them on your story, okay? You're lucky you have me as your personal assistant for the day." He said, and I chuckled as this was very new coming from him.

I looked at my parents; they were talking to each other. They were not saying much, but I could feel what they were feeling. I always imagined how it will be when Yohanne will come back. How will I tell him that I love him? How will he respond? Will he find me pretty? Will he fall in love with me then? There will be an awkwardness between us.

"Are you okay?" Rahil asked. "Getting there." I replied. "Who is this guy, by the way?" he said, looking at Yohanne's painting. I didn't say anything. "Rebound?" he asked. I rolled my eyes and was about to walk away; he pulled me by my arm. "Stay." He said. I looked at his eyes; they were staring deep into mine, not furiously but gently, with love. "I'm not going anywhere." I said. "You are... you just don't know it yet." He said, leaving my arm. "It's a big day, and I'm so proud of you." He said and kissed my forehead. I smiled at him and took a deep breath as the situation was getting too heavy on me. "Thank you, Rahil, but please don't kiss me again or get so close to me in front of my parents." I requested, and he bowed to me. I never found him attractive, but today he had a different charm in his body language. I was confused if he always had it, and I missed noticing that because I was never into him. I blushed.

15 mins later, people started showing up, looking at my paintings. I was expecting some millionaire to secretly buy all my paintings, and in the end, it'll turn out to be Yohanne who became a millionaire in Canada. I laughed at my own imagination.

I looked around. It was all so perfect. My parents were talking, my first exhibition was finally happening. I had beautiful friends around me who loved me, and a guy that genuinely cared for me. There was a void in my chest; I wanted him to see this. I wanted him to be with me holding my hand when I take the first step towards my career.

I looked for Sumair as he had my phone. I saw him wandering around the gallery. "Sumair! Can I get my phone now?" I walked towards him. "No, you cannot. I've posted the picture of your art on your Instagram." He said, wrapping his arm around my neck. "Why not? Now, it's getting irritating, Sumair." I said, looking at him with my fake angry look. "Shhh, focus baby, focus. It's such a big day; you're gonna make money." He said and walked me to my area. We stood there for a good 2-3 minutes looking at Yohanne's painting.

"It's beautiful," he said, looking at the portrait. I turned my head towards him. "Can you buy it?" I asked him. "You know Ahilya, I can't," he said and took a long pause. "But just the way I let him go, you gotta let him go too." He said, and with each word that came out of his mouth, my eyes filled with tears. "Hmm, I will let him go." I said, holding back that one drop which was going to fall off my eyes. "You have Rahil now! Look at him; he is handsome, he is caring, and more importantly, he loves you." He said, holding on to my shoulders. "Yeah, yeah, I know," I whined. "Look at him, just look at him." I looked in his direction; he was talking to my mom. She seemed to like him. They knew each other, but they never spoke so much before. A smile appeared on my face. "See, would Yohanne ever do this? Why do you wanna be with someone who doesn't care about you? You should be with someone who gets excited to see you every day." He said, and it all made sense. I took a deep breath, I was looking at Rahil, he turned to look at me, and we smiled at each other.

My phone rang from Sumair's pocket. He pulled it out, and I saw an incoming video call from Kajal and Abhishek. "Now you have to give me my phone." I widened my eyes and gave him a look. "Yes, please love, take it." He handed me the phone. "Hiii!!!" Kajal screamed so loudly that pretty much everyone there could hear her. "Hi!! HOW ARE YOU?" I asked her and jumped in excitement; I knew she was super happy for me. "I'm good, I don't care about that, but your art, oh my god girl, they look amazing!! I wanna buy one." She said. "Yes, I'll share the link with you of this gallery; you can buy." I replied. "Cool, I'm buying your love then." She said. I slowly walked away from Sumair; I needed some privacy. "Umm, okay.. yes, sure, please." I was a little awkward hearing it, but I had to accept that he was my love, maybe is. "Kya hua, all okay?" she asked; she didn't know much about the whole situation. I could not tell her how we drifted apart, especially in the last one year. "Nothing!!!! It's awesome; thanks for calling!! I love you." I said, forcing a smile on my face. "Of course you are, Abhishek is at work, he wants me to wish you from his side, aswell. Take care, and we love you so much." She said and blew me a flying kiss. I smiled back, and we hung up the call.

I looked at the stories Sumair had been posting; he posted multiple stories. The 3rd story was a back shot of me and Rahil looking at the wall that had all my paintings. I was shocked that he posted not a single picture of Yohanne's portrait. I started scrolling through the list of people who had viewed the story of mine and Rahil's picture. Yohanne's name was right there. He had not reacted to the picture; clearly, he didn't care. My curiosity made me click on his picture. I could see a red circle around his profile picture; he had posted a story. I clicked on it. It was a picture of Yohanne with another girl. With a caption "new beginning." My heart sank. I was sucked back into the emotion of losing something so close to me. It got harder for me to breathe. I looked back, and Sumair saw me from away; he was talking to Ahaan. My eyes were full of tears, and he stood still. I wiped my face and ran to the washroom. I closed the door behind me and looked into the mirror; my mascara was slowly smudging, and my eyes were red. I tried taking deep breaths, but the pain kept increasing. "Ohh shit shit shit whyyyy," the tears kept rolling down my face. I looked at myself, at my reflection, and it made me cry even more. I looked at my phone and scrolled through his feed, searching for one picture of him. I found one and stared at it for as long as I could. I gathered my courage and decided that I needed to tell him how I felt. I could barely see my phone's screen.

Al: Hi Yohanne, I know we have drifted apart, a little more in the last one year. But I saw your story with the girl, I'm guessing she is your girlfriend, and I'm guessing that maybe you're not coming back. I was a little heartbroken when you didn't reply to my text on your birthday with the same excitement. But I gotta tell you something. It has been inside for way too long.

Al: I am in love with you Yohanne, and I was in love with you a little since the day I saw you. We were probably not meant to be, and I had accepted that but was not ready to let you go. Today you saw my story of my art exhibition and didn't think once that you should have texted.

Al: I am heartbroken, but I will be fine. And I will move on, but I had to tell you that I loved you, and now maybe it will be easier to let go.

I sent the last text and sat on the floor of that washroom. I kept my phone aside and covered my face with my hands. I took a deep breath and picked up my phone. I opened the messenger again to see if he had seen the text or not. They were still unread. I exhaled and got up. I took a tissue paper out and tapped it on my face to clear the smudged makeup. "It's a big day for you, Ahilya; you gotta save your smile." I smiled at my reflection and pulled the door. I walked out like nothing had happened. I walked to my wall and saw a golden plate that said "SOLD" beneath Yohannes portrait.

CHAPTER 22

Yohanne

"When are you going back to India to get your?" Dave asked. Mom gave him a look, and he stopped. He took a bite of his bread and waited for me to respond. I was sitting to his right, and Mom was sitting to his left with Jai. She had called me for dinner, but they didn't tell him it was to discuss my future.

"Look Yohanne, we did not plan your visit to Canada like this, but we supported you, and your mom gave you everything she could. Now I don't wanna make this dinner uncomfortable, but I hope you will return the money soon." He said and looked at mom to validate what he was saying. "Yohanne beta, take your time; we have a couple of years before Jai starts college." She said, trying to console me. "Yeah, umm, but I'm not going to India anytime sooner, so I was planning to get a job and pay you guys back." I said. I had put my fork down; it was steak for dinner, and I wasn't used to this type of food. "Your dad didn't leave you anything, son?" Dave asked, and my mom touched his shoulder, trying to refrain him from asking me that question. "He did! But I just wanted to save it till the fixed deposit matures, and I was planning to buy a house with that money." I said, affirmatively. "Sure, I wish you all the luck. So let's start job hunting as soon as possible." He patted my shoulders and gave me a smile. I forced a smile too. "Come on, finish your dinner."

I picked up my fork, although I didn't want to eat. I couldn't leave the food here; it wasn't my home. I stuffed it into my mouth. I looked at the Christmas tree that they have put in the living room; it wasn't fully visible, but I could see half of it and the lights reflecting on the corridor floor. "So tell me, are you seeing someone?" Mom asked, leaning towards me a little to show interest. "Umm, yeah, I am," I blushed and looked down. "Aww, who is she?" Mom asked. Jai smiled and looked at me; I smirked, and he looked away. "Her name is Ahilya." I said and choked on my saliva. "Pass him some water, Dave." Mom said, handing Dave the water bottle. He poured the water into my glass. "Are you okay?" Dave asked, and I just nodded. I coughed until my breath got normal. Jai looked confused, as a few days back, he did ask me about my girlfriend, and I had told him about Carol.

I took a deep breath; my eyes were all watery and red. A minute later, when everything settled. I looked around, and all the attention was here on me. I misjudged them; I never had a family, and for the first time, I was realizing what it meant to have a family. They will have your back; they will get selfish at times, no doubt, but they will always have your back. "Feeling better?" Dave asked. I looked at him and regretted every minute I stayed away from my dad. "Yeah, I am all okay." I said and smiled at them; they all sighed and continued eating. Jai raised his eyebrows at me. I shook my head slow enough for others to not notice it. "So who is this Ahilya? Is she in your college?" Mom asked. "Umm, sorry I took the wrong name; it's Carol." I clarified. "Sure Ross!" Jai commented. Dave spilled the water from his mouth and started laughing. Mom covered her mouth, and she started laughing as well. I looked at them and realized what Jai meant. We all were laughing for the next one minute.

After dinner, mom gave me a blanket and a pillow so that I could sleep on the couch. "You'll be comfortable here?" she asked, and I nodded without saying anything. I sat on the couch, and she gestured me to sit next to her. I sat next to her, and she rubbed my upper back slowly. "You miss Yash so much, don't you?" She asked. I couldn't look at her. "Leave it, Mom; I don't wanna discuss that." I replied; she kept looking at me. I turned my head to her and instantly looked down; I could not make eye contact with her. "I thought he forcefully took me away from you; why didn't you ever clear that it was never his fault?" I questioned. "You cant expect a mother to tell her son that she had to give him up because of her addiction" She said, I looked at her. "I'm sorry, but he is gone now.." I looked into her eyes; they looked in pain. "Did you love him?" I asked.

"Yess, Yohanne, I loved him a lot, more than you can imagine," she replied. Her words didn't make any sense to me. How can someone love someone so much yet learn to live without them and to love someone else. "Why did it end?" I asked her, trying to get my answers. "Because he didn't pick me when I needed him to," she said, and chills went down my spine. "You know, love is all about timings; you can love someone with all your heart, and they can love you back equally, and yet you might not end up together," she continued. "Isn't she Shraddha's daughter?" she asked. I looked at her, confused. "How do you know her?" I asked. "How can an ex-wife not recognize the current love on her ex-husband's funeral?" she replied with a sad smile on her face. "I spoke to her, I saw her in tears, I saw her break down and I handled her, I hugged her, Yash would've wanted the same. And trust me, I was glad he had someone, but the situation was way too confusing for me to understand... all I understood was that the woman loved him." She sighed. I didn't say much; I kept looking at the carpet, crawling my toes on the grey fur. "Yes, is it her, Shraddha's daughter, but it's history, Mom, after Dad's funeral, I could not tell her how I felt for her... she got so busy handling her mom, her parents got separated after that." I said and laid my back on the couch. Mom laid next to me too. "Must be very difficult for her..." she asked. "She is a strong girl, Mom! Very strong girl." I replied. "Are you happy with Carol?" she questioned again. "Yeah, but I never felt that way for anyone." "Not even Carol?" she asked. "Not really, Carol is extremely beautiful, but it's not there, Ahilya was something else." "Really?" "Yeah! Her smile could make anyone smile. Her hair was so beautiful like waves in a brown ocean." I said looking at the ceiling but not noticing a single thing about the ceiling. "And her eyes?" she asked. "Very beautiful brown eyes. They were shiny; I've never seen such shiny eyes." "Why are you with Carol, Yohanne?" she asked turning her head to me. "Because I like her and will marry her." I said, but I myself didn't believe my words. "You're clearly in love with Ahilya, even after 2 years." She sat straight, completely turned towards me. "But she is not..." I cleared, my tone got a little high. "How do you know?" she asked. "Just a feeling, and she never told me she did, so it's clear." I said. "You love her?" she asked. "Maybe." "Did you ever tell her that you love her?" she asked, and I had no answers. She pulled me in for a hug, "you know, there's always this one girl for every guy, and if you let her go, then it'll always be a compromise." She said hugging me. "Sleep, take the night to yourself." She said. I closed my eyes. I could see our society, that night when I saw her on her balcony, when she bumped into me. When she came to me when I was struggling. When she was in my arms. "I love you Ahilya!" I mumbled.

"Yohanne? Wanna have some coffee?" Dave woke me up; I could barely open my eyes. The blinders were up, and all the light was on my face. I saw Dave with two cups of coffee in hands. I got off my back and sat straight. "What's the plan for the day?" he asked. "Ah, I have to go to Carol's shop and help her with the Christmas tree." I replied. "It's almost Christmas, did she wait specially for you?" he asked. I didn't say anything. I took a sip of my coffee, trying to start my brain. "I'm confused." I said. "With what?" He asked. "Nothing..." I looked at him, "thanks for the coffee." I said and looked at him.

"im really sorry Yohanne for all that you had to go through, just know that you have a family here." He said. "Thanks Dave , I'll get going." I said. I kept the cup on the center table and got up. I walked towards my mom's room, then realized that I can't just leave my cups anywhere. I went back and saw Dave reaching for it. I picked it mid-way, "sorry, I just left it there; give me, I'll wash it." I said, he smiled at me and patted my shoulder. I went to the kitchen and washed the cup. I placed it in its place and felt good about myself. I walked up to my mom's room. I opened the door, and she was there on her bed, sleeping peacefully. I felt grateful that I at least had her. Gave her a kiss on her forehead, she opened her eyes and saw me, "Good morning MOM." I said with a smile. "Good morning Yohanne." She placed her hand on my cheeks and stared at my face with a smile on her face.

"I have therapy in 2 hours; I will go there and after that, I'll quickly help Carol with the tree and I'll come back for dinner?" I asked. "Yes! Please come." She said, sitting up on her bed. "I can sleep on the couch!" I said, and she chuckled. I laughed too. "I'll go now." I kissed her on her cheek and turned quickly to leave. "Yohanne!" she called me from behind. I turned back to hear what she had to say. "Your phone is charged? You don't need it?" she picked the phone from her side table; I had forgotten about my phone completely "opps, I forgot." I said and took it from her hand. "You're the first Gen-Z who doesn't care about his phone." She stated. "Bye, ma!" I said and left. "I love you!!" she yelled from behind. "Love you too"

I yelled back, crossing the living areas; Dave was sitting there watching TV "Bye Dave!" I waved at him quickly while leaving. "Bye Yohanne, See you for dinner!" He said. My heart felt full, I left their place and checked the time on my phone. There were multiple missed calls from Carol and three messages from Ahilya. My heart skipped a beat. I closed my eyes once before opening the text; I could hear my heartbeat in my ears. I exhaled to calm myself. I kept walking slowly. I clicked on the notification.

Al: Hi Yohanne, I know we have drifted apart, a little more in the last one year. But I saw your story with the girl; I'm guessing she is your girlfriend, and I'm guessing that maybe you're not coming back. I was a little heartbroken when you didn't reply to my text on your birthday with the same excitement. But I gotta tell you something. It has been inside for way too long.

Al: I am in love with you Yohanne, and I was in love with you a little since the day I saw you; we were probably not meant to be, and I had accepted that but was not ready to let you go. Today you saw my story of my art exhibition and didn't think once that you should have texted.

Al: I am heartbroken but I will be fine. And I will move on, but I had to tell you that I loved you and now maybe it will be easier to let go.

CHAPTER 23

Ahilya

"He did not even see the text yet, Reply toh dur ki baat hai," I said to Sumair while walking. "It's okay, you wanted to tell him, you did, you are free now," Sumair replied. "Hmm, maybe I am." I smiled at him. "Are you excited for the date?" he asked. "Nervous, more than excited," I replied. "It's okay, calm down, love. He deserves a chance; he will prove it to you. I'm sure that he is the right choice; I've seen it in his eyes, the way he loves you." "Thank you so much for being there for me." I hugged him, looked at the Café. "Coffee Craft," I sighed. I walked in, and the place was filled with the aroma of coffee. I looked back, and Sumair waved at me, I waved back at him and walked inside. Rahil was sitting in the same spot. "Hi!" he said and came forward to hug me. I hugged him back. "Why did you pick this place?" I asked him. "After you left, I started hating this place, but now that you're back, I don't want to keep hating this place," he said, holding his hand out. I hesitated for a bit, but then I gave him my hand. He slowly kissed it. I looked at his face. "You look really good." I said, he looked up and smiled. "Still, you left me." He said sarcastically, I giggled. "But I'm glad you acknowledged my beauty." He said, checking himself out in the glass window of the café. I laughed at it. "Hmm, I've missed you so much Ahilya!" He said, placing his hand on mine. I didn't feel much when he did that, like the sensitivity was gone from my hand. "So what do you wanna order?" he asked. "Hmm, I'll have a hazelnut frappe." I said looking at the menu. "I'll go get it right now." He said and got up from his seat, turned back to look at me and smiled. I smiled back at him. It just didn't feel right. I looked at my phone, yet, no reply from Yohanne. There was a text from Sumair.

SUMAIR- Don't think much, one day you'll realize you made the right choice. Al – Hmm

I locked my phone and looked at Rahil; he looked so happy. I wanted him to stay that way. I didn't know what Yohanne felt for me, but I knew for sure that Rahil loved me as much as I loved Yohanne. He turned with the tray and started walking towards me. He came closer, and the smile on his face kept getting bigger and bigger. A smile appeared on my face too; I didn't need Yohanne in my life; I had Rahil. He placed the tray on the table. I picked my glass and took a sip from it. "Do you like it?" he asked. "Yes, it's very good." I took another sip from the straw. "So Ahilya... I just wanted to ask something." He said, looking at me with wide eyes. "Ask.." I said. "Would you like to continue dating me?" he asked. "Yeah, I would." I said, and he blushed. "Are we back again?" he asked. "I think so, yeah!!" I said; his smile got bigger. "Okay, where do you wanna go next?" he asked. "Okay, what about a good expensive restaurant?" I replied. "Perfect, done!! What about tonight?" he asked. "Okay, you're paying!" I said. "Yes, mi lady, I will." He said and took my hand and kissed it. It made me blush a little.

That night I was getting ready in my room. My mom knocked. I looked at her; I was wearing a black bodycon dress. "You look so pretty, Ahilya!" she said from outside, "come in na" I said; she walked in and stood behind me. "Are you happy?" she asked. "Absolutely! Rahil is so perfect." I replied, and I did believe every word I said; he was perfect. "Okay than great, have a great night." She said hugging me from behind. "Will you get back with Dad?" I asked. "I don't know that Ahilya, maybe.. maybe not.." she said. "I hope you guys do." I said, "I'll go now; Rahil will be down any minute now." "Yes, yes, please go!" she said. I walked out of my house, and she was at the door, seeing me go for my date. Not the one that I wanted but the one that I needed. The lift opened, and I entered. My phone rang; I expected Rahil. I looked at my phone, and it was Yohanne. I picked.

"Hello?" I said. "He..." his voice was breaking a lot. "Hello Yohanne, I'm in the lift, I'll call you back." I said. "No, wait." He said. "I'm in the lift; I can't hear anything." I said. Finally, the lift opened on the ground floor. "Yes, tell me." I asked him while walking out of the building. "Hey.. I'm coming back."

SHARE YOUR PERFECT STRANGER MOMENT

_____

_____

_____

_____

_____

_____

_____

_____

_____

_____

_____

_____

_____

www.ingramcontent.com/pod-product-compliance
Lightning Source LLC
LaVergne TN
LVHW061544070526
838199LV00077B/6898